Tales of King Arthur

Retold by Felicity Brooks

Introduction by Anna Claybourne

Illustrations by
Rodney Matthews

First published in 2002 by Usborne Publishing Ltd,
Usborne House, 83-85 Saffron Hill, London
EC1N 8RT, England.
www.usborne.com

Edited by Anthony Marks
Series editors: Jane Chisholm and Rosie Dickins
Designed by Brian Voakes
Series designer: Mary Cartwright
Cover design by Sonia Dobie
Cover photographs © Yann Layma/Getty Images
With special thanks to Christian Fletcher,
Ed Kazakewich & Brad Beniot

Printed in Great Britain

JFMAMJ ASOND/10 00347/1

CONTENTS

About King Arthur

King Arthur is a legendary king of Britain who has appeared in stories and folk tales ever since medieval times (about 1000-1500). He is supposed to have lived in the Dark Ages, which is a name for the time after the Romans left Britain, between about 400 and 700. He is said to have been a heroic leader who fought off invaders and successfully conquered many lands. Stories about him have gradually become more and more elaborate over the years.

Although many of the stories about King Arthur have been made up by writers and storytellers, they may still be based on a real, historical person. Some medieval historians wrote about a general or chieftain called Arthur, who died in a battle in about 540, along with someone called Medraut, who may be the person behind the character of Mordred in the stories.

Legendary tales of Arthur and his knights first began to appear in the 12th century, when a British historian, Geoffrey of Monmouth, wrote about Arthur in a book called *The History of the Kings of Britain*. However, although this was described as a history book, it was probably, in fact, mostly made up! Geoffrey's version includes Merlin the magician,

Guinevere, Mordred and "Walwain" (another name for Gawain).

Later, the stories were developed into much longer versions by other writers, including a French writer named Chrétien de Troyes, and the legends began to spread throughout Europe. Then, in the 15th century, an English knight, Sir Thomas Malory, translated the tales from French back into English, in a very long book called *Le Morte D'Arthur* (*The Death of Arthur*). Malory is thought to have written *Le Morte D'Arthur* while he was serving a long prison sentence. Despite its title, it tells the story of Arthur's whole life, as well as many of the adventures of the Knights of the Round Table. Many of the tales in this book are based on Malory's stories.

Many writers through the ages have retold the legends of King Arthur. For example, in the 19th century, the poet Alfred Tennyson wrote about Arthur in his poem *The Idylls of the King*. *The Sword in the Stone,* by T. H. White, is a novel about Arthur's childhood. Many stories of King Arthur's life have been made into films and cartoons.

Although no one really knows whether the Round Table existed, or where Camelot or Avalon were, there are still some parts of Britain that are particularly connected with the legend of King Arthur. Some people say he is buried at Glastonbury Tor, in Somerset, southern England. You can also visit Tintagel, in Cornwall, where he is supposed to have been born. Many of the other places mentioned in this book, such as Carlisle, the Wirral, Orkney and Kent, are real parts of Britain.

The sword in the stone

"Please can I come with you?" begged Arthur. "Please?"

He was watching his father and brother as they saddled their horses. They were about to go to a tournament, and Arthur was determined not to be left out. It had to be worth just one more try.

"I promise I won't get in the way, and I'll sharpen your weapons and shine up your armor and look after the horses," he said, trying a direct appeal to his father. Sir Ector, who was busy loading the saddlebags, did not look up.

"You can't go," said Kay dismissively. "You're not even a knight."

Kay, or rather Sir Kay, as Arthur now had to call him, had just been knighted, and he took great delight in reminding his brother of this fact. Now, after years of training, he was at last allowed to take part in a real tournament. His sword was razor-sharp, his brand-new armor had been polished to perfection, and he could hardly wait to show off his jousting skills. The last thing he wanted was his little brother tagging along behind him.

"But you'll need a squire," said Arthur. "Please let me be your squire."

Sir Ector glanced down at Arthur's earnest, expectant face. There were good reasons why he didn't want him to go. He wished he could explain. But then, what harm could it really do?

"Well, Arthur, I suppose you might be useful. . ."

"But Father!" protested Kay. Ector ignored him.

"And you'll be a knight yourself soon, so this will be a chance for you to learn how to behave. But one hint of trouble. . ."

"You won't even know I'm there," grinned Arthur. He was already packing his bag. Kay shot him a filthy look and was still muttering under his breath when they set off.

The tournament had been arranged for New Year's Day, and people were coming from far and wide to take part or watch. Knights with their squires, dukes and earls, ladies on horseback, barons with their servants, whole families of peasants, wandering minstrels, shepherds, beggars, butchers, bakers, candlestickmakers and hordes of other curious onlookers thronged the muddy road, all heading for the town where the tournament was to take place. Ector soon realized that they'd have little chance of finding a place to stay unless one of them went ahead.

"I'll go," said Arthur. "I'll try the Blue Boar Inn first, and if there's no room there, I'll leave a message to say where I've gone."

"All right," said Ector. "We'll meet you there. Ride safely!"

Arthur charged off at full gallop.

As soon as he was out of earshot, Ector turned to Kay conspiratorially.

"I think you should know that this isn't just any old tournament," he said.

"What do you mean?" asked Kay.

"Well, the story I've heard is that the Archbishop has arranged it for a particular purpose."

"And what's that?"

"To find the new king," said Ector.

Kay looked confused.

"Well, you know that since King Uther died (it must be over thirteen years ago now) the kingdom's been in complete chaos. There was no known successor to the throne, so all the knights and barons have been squabbling among themselves. And to make matters worse, King Uther's old enemies have invaded parts of the kingdom." Ector paused and pulled his cloak around him. The afternoon air was growing colder as the weak, winter sun began to set.

"Well, apparently," continued Ector, "an old sorcerer came out of his hiding place in Wales just before Christmas and told the Archbishop to summon all the nobles to a big service in the cathedral. He said there would be a miracle which would reveal the true heir to the throne. Well, the Archbishop adores miracles, so he did what the old sorcerer said.

"On Christmas morning, the nobles all packed into the cathedral. In fact, I've heard there wasn't enough room for everybody inside, so some of them spilled out into the square. The service started and the Archbishop was about to give one of his long, boring sermons, when all of a sudden there was some shouting outside. Everybody immediately piled out into the square to see what all the noise was about."

Ector stopped for a moment to read a milestone at the side of the road. They still had some way to go.

"And what was the noise about?" asked Kay impatiently.

"I'm just coming to that," said Ector. He spurred his horse on and then coughed to clear his throat.

"When they got outside they saw a strange block of stone. Nobody knew where it had come from. It had just appeared as if from nowhere. Sticking out of the stone was the handle of a very large sword. They all crowded around for a closer look and saw carved into the stone the message:

WHOEVER PULLS THIS SWORD OUT
OF THIS STONE IS THE TRUE
BORN KING OF LOGRES.

"Well, of course, all the knights started jostling to take turns to pull the sword out. One after another, they leaped up onto the block, heaving and straining, puffing and panting and moaning and groaning until they were red in the face. But not even the strongest knight could budge the sword an inch. It was as if the metal and the stone had been fused together.

"Well, finally the Archbishop decided that the trueborn king was not there. And that was when he had the idea for this tournament, as a way of bringing all the nobles in the land together to have a try at jousting and to take a turn with the sword. That way, he'd be sure to find the king. So he quickly chose some messengers to ride around the kingdom to tell people about the sword in the stone, and picked out ten knights to guard it."

"So. . . will I get the chance to pull the sword out?" asked Kay.

"Well, yes, if we can get anywhere near it with all this excitement," said Ector.

By now, they were approaching the town walls. People were streaming in through the gates and surging along the narrow, cobbled streets. Ector and Kay made their way through the crowd to the cathedral square. A large mob had gathered around the stone. The guards were letting knights through, one by one, to try to pull the sword out. Kay wanted to try immediately, but Ector stopped him.

"There'll be plenty of time for that tomorrow," he said. "Now we should see what Arthur's up to."

"He'd better have found us a place to stay," growled

Kay threateningly.

Arthur didn't disappoint them. He'd managed to find some small rooms at the Blue Boar, which was only a couple of miles from the tournament ground. They ate some supper and went straight to bed. The tournament was due to start early the following morning.

Kay woke up feeling nervous, so nervous, in fact, that he forgot to put on his sword. He didn't discover this until they were already well on their way to the tournament. He blamed Arthur and told him to ride back to fetch it.

Arthur galloped off at once. But when he arrived back at the inn, he found the heavy front door locked and bolted. He pounded on the wood with his fists, but no one answered. He went to each of the ground floor windows and yelled through the shutters, but there was no reply. Everybody had gone to the tournament.

"Where on earth am I going to get a sword from now?" he wailed miserably. "Kay will kill me if I go back without one."

Frustrated and despondent, he rode through the deserted town, and was still thinking about what to do when he passed in front of the cathedral. Something glinting in the sunlight caught his eye. He trotted over to investigate.

"The answer to my prayers..." he told himself, seeing a very large sword sticking out of a big block of stone. The square was empty. The guards had all abandoned their posts to go to the tournament.

Without bothering to stop and read the inscription, Arthur clambered up, grasped the handle of the sword in both hands and gave it a sharp tug. As smoothly and silently as a snake leaving its burrow, the shining blade slid from the stone.

Arthur stood for a moment, staring at his amazing find, before glancing around quickly to make sure he wasn't being watched. Then he leaped down and sliced the crisp, morning air with the sparkling blade in a furious, imaginary fight. Then he remembered that the tournament was about to begin, so he hid the sword under his cloak and galloped back as fast as he could.

"Here's a sword," he said, holding it out to Kay. "I couldn't get yours, but. . ."

Kay recognized the sword immediately, and before Arthur could finish his sentence he had snatched it from him, tucked it under his own cloak and rushed off to find Sir Ector.

"Look what I've done," Kay said excitedly, when he found him. "It's the sword from the stone. I pulled it out. I must be the trueborn king."

Sir Ector gave Kay a quizzical look.

"Well, if you can do it once, you can do it again,

and this time you'll have an audience," he said calmly. He insisted that they all ride straight back to the cathedral, even though he knew that meant they would miss the tournament. And every time Arthur opened his mouth to try to tell Ector what had really happened, Kay silenced him with a menacing glare. Back at the cathedral, Ector marched them straight to the stone.

"Now, put the sword back exactly where you found it, Kay," he said. Kay jumped up onto the stone and tried to thrust the sword into it, but failed miserably.

"It's strange that you could pull it out, but you can't put it back," said Ector.

Kay climbed down, shamefaced.

"Now tell me where you really got it," said Ector.

"From Arthur," admitted Kay, not daring to look his father in the eye.

"And where did you get it from?" Ector asked patiently, turning to Arthur.

"From the stone, I promise," babbled Arthur. "I tried to get Kay's sword, but the door at the inn was locked, and. . . I knew he'd be cross, and I saw this sword and I. . . I didn't want him to miss the tournament, so I took it and I. . ."

"Calm down, Arthur," said Ector. "Now let's see if you can put it back."

Arthur took the sword from Kay and climbed up onto the stone. The blade slid back in, like a warm knife into butter. Sir Ector then climbed up next to him and tried to pull it out. He failed.

"Now it's your turn, Kay," he said. Kay jumped up and seized the handle. He pulled and yanked and heaved, but had no more luck than his father. Finally, Arthur, still unable to see what all the fuss was about, climbed up, grabbed the handle and once more effortlessly pulled the sword from the stone. When he looked down, much to his surprise, his father and brother were kneeling in front of him, heads bowed.

"What are you doing?" he asked.

"Kneeling before our king," Ector replied. "Read the words on the stone, Arthur, and you'll see that there's only one person alive who can pull out this sword, and he's our trueborn king."

Arthur started to feel dizzy and slightly faint. He read the words over and over again until they swam in front of his eyes. It must be a mistake. . . or somebody was playing a trick on him. How could he be the king? He wasn't even a knight, nor from a royal family. His head started to spin. Then he felt a reassuring hand on his shoulder.

"Sit down, Arthur," said Ector. "There are a few things I need to tell you, but it's hard to know where to start."

"At the beginning?" suggested Arthur, sitting on a low wall.

"At the beginning," sighed Ector, as he sat down next to him. "This is going to be a shock for you, Arthur, but you had to know someday."

Ector took a deep breath, before launching into the

story he'd been dreading having to tell. . .

"The night of your birth, Arthur, there was a terrible storm. Huge waves lashed the rocks, the wind howled and the roads became rivers overnight. I remember it well, because shortly after midnight there was a knock on the door. Outside, huddled against the biting wind, was a hunched, ragged figure, cradling something under his cloak. I knew exactly who he was and why he was there. It was Merlin, the sorcerer, disguised as a beggar, and the bundle he was carrying was a tiny, newborn child. He had climbed down the secret cliff path from Tintagel Castle, just before it was cut off by the tide, and scrambled along the beach in the driving rain. The baby, wrapped in a gold cloth, was the son of King Uther Pendragon and Duchess Igrayne."

Sir Ector paused for a moment to see how much of this story Arthur was taking in, but it was impossible to tell. The boy's head was lowered and his eyes were fixed firmly on his feet.

"You see, King Uther had a great many enemies and Merlin had told him that if the infant stayed at the castle, his young life would be in danger. So Merlin arranged to bring the baby to us in secret. He told us to raise him as our own son, and said that we should call him Arthur."

Sir Ector paused again. Arthur was staring at him with a puzzled look on his face.

"So I'm not really your son," he said slowly, in disbelief. "And Kay, he's not really my. . ." Ector quickly cut in.

"I didn't want to have to tell you this, Arthur. I've always thought of you as my own son. I tried to forget

about what happened that night, though I knew the story would come out one day, when Merlin thought the time was right. When I heard about the sword in the stone, I did my best to stop you from finding out about it, but I knew the time had come. Merlin had arranged it."

"That's why I didn't want you to come with us. I couldn't bear to lose you. . ." His voice trailed off. It was Arthur's turn to speak:

"But, even if this is true, and I am the trueborn king, I'll always think of you as my father, and Kay will always be my brother, however mean he's been to me," he added.

There was a painfully long silence.

"What happened to my real mother and father?" Arthur asked, eventually.

"Your father was poisoned by one of his enemies when you were only two years old," said Ector solemnly, "but I believe your mother is still alive, and you have a sister, named Anna, and a half-sister."

There were still so many questions Arthur wanted to ask, but he had to wait until they had more time. There were many important tasks to attend to. First of all, they had to decide what to do about the sword. They made an appointment to see the Archbishop that same day to explain what had happened. As soon as he had seen Arthur removing the sword again, the Archbishop made an official announcement that the trueborn king had been found, and rushed off to get ready for the coronation.

Most of the knights roared with laughter when they heard that Arthur was heir to the throne, refusing to believe that this shy young man, who wasn't even a knight, could possibly be their ruler. Only a few nobles who had survived from the days of King Uther, and who recognized the family likeness, swore their allegiance. The rest were scornful. They dispersed reluctantly, muttering that the whole thing had been fixed and that they'd never swear loyalty to this unknown upstart.

So the Archbishop had no choice but to arrange some more tournaments: four, in fact, for Twelfth Night, Candlemas, Easter and Whitsun, when once again, anyone who wanted could have a turn at removing the sword. On each occasion, of all the hundreds of knights, dukes, barons, earls and ordinary people who tried to remove the sword, only Arthur was successful.

At the Whitsun tournament, when he had accomplished the feat for the final time, a loud cheer went up from the huge crowd that had gathered to watch the spectacle.

"We want Arthur!" someone shouted. "Arthur for king!" yelled another. Then a murmur started at the back of the crowd. Little by little, the murmur grew to a rumble, and the rumble to a roar. It was the sound of a demand that could not be refused.

"WE WANT ARTHUR! WE WANT ARTHUR! WE WANT ARTHUR!" chanted the crowd, stamping their feet and drowning out the groans of a portly baron who had hauled himself onto the stone and was desperately straining to dislodge the sword. Shepherds were banging their crooks on the ground, tinkers were clanging their pots, children were clapping their hands, dogs were barking, and even the Archbishop found himself tapping his toes in time to the rhythm.

"WE WANT ARTHUR! WE WANT ARTHUR! WE WANT ARTHUR!" The huge uproar continued unabated, until at last even the most stubborn knights realized that, incredible as it might seem, Arthur must be their true and rightful king.

Row after row of knights, lords and ladies dropped to their knees to swear loyalty to Arthur, and begged his forgiveness for having delayed his succession for so long. Arthur passed among them, shaking hands with them and accepting their apologies. When the clamor finally died down, the Archbishop stepped forward and announced that the king would be knighted immediately. Arthur was carried jubilantly into the cathedral and people crammed the aisles to see the Archbishop knight him with the sword from the stone.

A few days later, King Arthur was crowned, amid rejoicing and celebration. The new king promised to

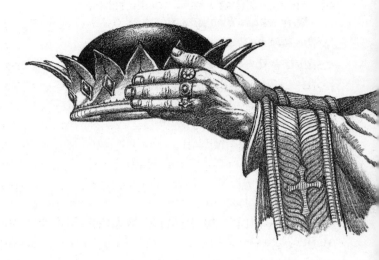

rule justly over his people, to right all wrongs, to drive out the invaders, and to bring peace and prosperity to the troubled Kingdom of Logres. After the ceremony, there was a noisy procession through the streets, with the crowds cheering their new leader along.

Unseen at the back of the crowd stood a mysterious, bearded figure in a long cloak. At first, Arthur was unaware of him. But then, as if from nowhere, he suddenly heard a deep, resonant voice echoing inside his head:

"*Many who scorn you
soon will serve you.
Many called friends will
one day be enemies.
Yours is a time of wonder,
a time of triumph,
a time of magic.
Rule wisely, King Arthur.
You are destined for
eternal greatness.*"

Arthur looked all around to see where the voice had come from, but Merlin had already vanished into the night.

Excalibur

King Arthur never forgot the solemn vow he made on the day he was crowned, but it was no easy task to bring peace to the Kingdom of Logres. The land he now ruled had been torn apart by year after year of struggle and strife, and his father's old enemies seemed to be everywhere. His subjects were weary of long, bitter battles and worn down by the hardship and misery they had endured during those dark, troubled days.

Soon after his coronation, Arthur gathered an army and drove out the invaders. He restored all the stolen land to its rightful owners, and set about building castles to defend all the coasts and borders of the kingdom.

As soon as this had been done, Arthur summoned together his most loyal knights and followers and set up court at Camelot, the biggest and most beautiful castle in all of Logres. It was at Camelot that he was finally reunited with his real mother, Igrayne, his sister, Anna, and his half-sister, Morgan le Fay, a powerful sorceress who had learned all her magic from Merlin.

Despite all the joy and excitement of meeting his real family, Arthur didn't forget Ector and Kay. Each member of his foster family was given an honorary position in the new royal household.

One morning, about a year into Arthur's reign, a bedraggled squire rode into the courtyard at Camelot on a shambling horse. Hobbling behind him was another horse, with the bloodied body of the squire's master, Sir Miles, slumped across its saddle. The boy was so upset he could hardly speak, and it was some time before he had calmed down enough to explain what had happened.

He described how he and his master had been trotting through the forest when Sir Miles had been attacked by a knight named Sir Pellinore. Sir Pellinore was a formidable fighter. He liked nothing better than to boast about how many knights he had killed. And now he had set up his tent by a well near the road, and would not let anyone pass unless they jousted with him first.

When the tearful young squire had finished this story, he flung himself to his knees and begged King Arthur to help him avenge the death of his master. Arthur, moved by the young man's plight, was considering what to do when Gryflet, a squire of the court, strode forward and volunteered to face Sir Pellinore himself.

"You're much too young, Gryflet," Arthur told him, ". . . and no match for Sir Pellinore. You'll be an excellent knight when you're older, and I don't want to lose you now."

But Gryflet continued to plead with such persistence that eventually Arthur relented. He told Gryflet that he would knight him and let him ride out to the forest only if he promised to joust with Pellinore just once, and then come straight back to Camelot. Gryflet eagerly agreed, and quickly knelt down to be knighted. Then he put on his armor, seized his weapons and charged across the drawbridge. But in no time he was back, clinging feebly to his horse's neck, with a deep spear wound in his side.

Arthur was furious. By the time a surgeon arrived, he was galloping out of the gates himself, fully armed and with his heart set on revenge. When he reached the edge of the forest, a boy of about fourteen suddenly stepped out into the road in front of him.

"Whoa!" yelled the boy, raising his hand. Arthur

brought his horse to an abrupt halt.

"Why do you look so serious?" asked the boy with a sly grin.

"Because of the things I've seen," said Arthur, surprised by the question.

"I know that already," snapped the boy. "In fact, I know everything you're thinking and I know that you're a fool."

Arthur could hardly believe his ears, but the boy went on undaunted:

"And I know your mother and I knew your father, King Uther, and. . . "

"You little liar!" yelled Arthur. "You've got no idea what you're talking about. You're far too young to know any of this. Now get out of my sight."

The boy sidled off into the forest and almost at once an old man with a long purple cloak appeared in his place. His face looked kind and wise.

"Why do you look so serious, sir?" the old man asked in a sonorous voice.

Not again, thought Arthur. "Because I've just met an insolent boy who called me a fool and said that he knew my father," was his reply.

"But he did know your father," insisted the old man. "And he knows many other things about you. He knows that one day your kingdom will fall to a child who is not yet born, and that the same child will grow up to defeat you in battle, and that the child will be named Mordred, and. . . "

"Stop!" said Arthur. "Who are you to tell me this?"

"Merlin," said the old man, and before Arthur's eyes he changed back into the boy. Then, just as suddenly, he vanished into thin air with an eerie little laugh that rang through the forest. Arthur looked around, but he was completely alone.

"Merlin!" called Arthur. "Come back. I need to talk to you." But Merlin had gone.

Arthur had heard countless stories about Merlin. He even recognized his voice, but it was the first time they'd met face to face since the day he was born. He continued slowly along the road, pondering the prophecies Merlin had made. He hadn't gone much further when he saw the old man again, sprinting frantically through the trees, his cloak billowing behind him. Hard on his heels ran three evil-looking thugs. Arthur charged after them, brandishing his sword and shouting at the top of his voice. The thugs bolted into the forest.

"Your magic couldn't save you this time, old man," said Arthur.

"It could have done," the sorcerer replied casually, not even pausing for breath, "more than your anger will save you when you meet Sir Pellinore."

Merlin mounted his horse, which was grazing at the side of the road, and accompanied Arthur on his journey to face Sir Pellinore. Arthur fired questions at him all the way, but Merlin simply refused to answer any of them.

When they reached the well, they saw Sir Pellinore,

fully armed and grim-faced, sitting on a huge horse in front of his tent. Arthur gulped, suddenly feeling very nervous.

"Sir Pellinore. . . ?" he asked hesitantly. The menacing figure said nothing.

"Sir Pellinore," Arthur repeated, "I've been told that you're stopping people from passing along this road." Pellinore turned slowly in his saddle and fixed Arthur with a belligerent stare.

"That's true," he said tersely.

"Well, I've come to demand that you change your

ways," said Arthur, trying to sound important and doing his best to disguise the wobble in his voice.

"You'll just have to force me, then, won't you?" said Sir Pellinore, gripping his lance and turning his horse around, ready to joust.

Sighing, Arthur clapped down his visor. This knight was obviously not in the mood for a discussion.

They jousted three times, charging fearlessly across the clearing and clashing their lances together. The horses panted and steamed as their sharp hooves pounded the dewy grass into mud. The first and second time, both of the lances broke and neither knight could gain an advantage. But the third time the opponents clashed together, Sir Pellinore swung his lance into exactly the right position, and Arthur was knocked off his horse. He leaped to his feet, abandoned his lance and whipped his sword from its scabbard.

"You may be better at jousting," he shouted bravely, "but let's see what you can do on foot."

Pellinore dismounted. Reluctant though he was to relinquish the advantage he had gained on horseback, the rules of chivalry had to be obeyed. They fought long and hard until both of them collapsed, breathless with pain and exhaustion. Their armor was dented, and blood trickled onto the grass, but neither fighter would give in.

Merlin leaned on his staff at the edge of the clearing, watching impassively as the two men staggered to their feet and the fighting started again. Once more the clash of swords and the groans of the duellers echoed through the forest, until Arthur's sword snapped in two.

"Surrender or die!" panted Pellinore.

"Never!" screamed Arthur, dropping the broken sword. He rushed at Pellinore full tilt, grabbed him around the waist and knocked him down to the ground. Pellinore fought like a wild cat to release himself, until, with a blood-curdling cry, he overturned Arthur, clambered on top of him and pinned him down on the grass.

Arthur stared up into the big knight's frenzied face, struggling desperately to free himself from the vice-like grip of his enemy. But he wasn't strong enough. Pellinore wrenched off Arthur's helmet, raised his heavy sword above his head, and was just about to bring the blade down on Arthur's neck to deliver the fatal blow, when Merlin muttered a hasty spell. Pellinore's eyes clamped shut. His sword fell from his hand and he toppled slowly forward.

"Have you killed him?" asked Arthur breathlessly, easing himself out from under the lifeless body. "Merlin, is he dead?"

"No," replied the magician, casually prodding the body with his staff. "He's just asleep. Actually he's in much better shape than you are." Arthur by now was slumped on the ground, moaning, and bleeding badly from several wounds.

"You're going to need good fighters like him, and

he'll live to serve you well," said Merlin. "His son Percival is going to be one of the bravest Knights of the Round Table."

Arthur was too weak and exhausted to take any of this in, or to ask the sorcerer what he meant. Merlin helped him climb onto his horse, and they set off again into the woods, leaving Sir Pellinore lying on the muddy grass, among the wreckage of broken weapons and armor.

Merlin led the way to a cottage deep in the forest which was the home of an ancient healer. The old man treated Arthur's wounds with herbal lotions, and after three days he was well enough to ride again. They thanked the healer and left.

"I wish I hadn't broken my sword," said Arthur as they were riding through the forest.

"Don't worry," said Merlin, "you'll soon have another that will last forever. It'll be the best sword in the world, forged in the depths of Lake Avalon."

Once again, Arthur had no idea what Merlin was talking about. But the old magician always seemed to know exactly what was going to happen, so he said nothing. And at that moment, they trotted out of the shadow of the trees into bright sunshine. A gleaming expanse of water lay before them, with a huge, purple mountain rising up behind it.

Arthur scanned the lake's silvery surface, and without knowing why, he found his eyes coming to rest on a spot in the middle. Without any warning, a hand suddenly shot up from beneath the water, holding a jewel-covered sword and scabbard, which sparkled in the sunlight.

"Look over there!" shouted Arthur in amazement. "Look at that sword!"

"That's Excalibur, Arthur. It's the sword you will carry to the end of your days."

Arthur jumped down from his saddle and waded into the water as if drawn to the sword by some magical force. A fine mist was rolling down the mountainside and rapidly covering the lake.

"Look," said Merlin, pointing across the water. A tall woman in a long robe was gliding across the surface towards them.

"That's the Lady of the Lake," Merlin whispered. "If you want to own Excalibur, you must do exactly what she says."

The Lady of the Lake was now right in front of them, hovering just above the still, misty water. Arthur stared at her in disbelief.

"King Arthur," she said in a deep, gentle voice, "Excalibur will be yours if you agree to do whatever I ask in the future."

"I will do whatever it is in my power to do," said Arthur, intent only on getting hold of the sword as soon as possible. "I promise," he added hurriedly.

"Then use my barge," said the Lady, gesturing

towards an ornate boat, half-hidden among the reeds
at the side of the lake.

Arthur needed no more encouragement. He raced
along the shore, stepped into the boat and pushed out
into the deep, dark water. The barge drifted silently
across the lake, parting the carpet of mist before it.
When it reached the middle, Arthur stretched out and
plucked the sword and scabbard from the fairy hand.
At once, the little arm disappeared back into the water.

Excalibur was the most beautiful weapon Arthur
had ever seen. He was so lost in admiration that he was

unaware of the boat floating gently back to the shore, or of the Lady of the Lake vanishing into the still water. By the time he looked back, the surface was as smooth and calm as before.

Merlin and Arthur started back through the forest. When they reached the well, they saw the mighty Sir Pellinore lying asleep, just as they had left him. But all of his wounds were now healed.

"I won't wake him yet," said Merlin, "but I can guarantee he won't give you any more trouble."

"That's a shame," replied Arthur, "because now I have Excalibur, I'd like to fight him again, and this time I'd win."

"Don't be so sure," said Merlin wisely, shaking his head at the young king's haste. "He's still a stronger fighter than you are. Anyway, there'll be plenty of opportunity to use Excalibur very soon indeed."

Arthur drew the sword out of its scabbard once more, so that he could admire it again.

"Which of them do you like best?" asked Merlin. "The sword itself, or the scabbard?"

"The sword, definitely," said Arthur, gazing in awe at the heavy, razor-sharp silver blade, and tracing with his fingers the strange patterns carved into the sword's richly jewelled hilt.

"Then you're a fool," said Merlin bluntly, "because

the scabbard is enchanted, and it's worth much more than the sword. While you're wearing that scabbard, you'll never lose a drop of blood, however badly you're injured."

"That's the second time you've called me a fool," Arthur pointed out, although he realized that what Merlin had just told him made the sword even more precious than he had imagined.

Their horses were now trudging up a slope on the final approach to Camelot, and the sun was just setting.

"Well, I may be a fool," the king announced at last, grinning at Merlin, "but now I'm a fool with the best sword in the world."

Then, laughing with excitement and holding Excalibur high in the air, he spurred on his horse to gallop the last stretch home to Camelot.

The gathering of the knights

Merlin sighed, folded his arms and looked straight into Arthur's face. Arthur had just told the ancient sorcerer that he wanted to marry Guinevere, the beautiful daughter of King Leodegrance.

"You're making a mistake," he said slowly and solemnly. "A big mistake."

"But I. . ." protested Arthur. Merlin cut in sharply:

"I know she's probably the most charming and beautiful woman you've ever met, and you no doubt believe that you're in love with her, but it's exactly that which will bring about the destruction of all that is important to you. I beg you to think again. Does it have to be Guinevere?"

"Yes," said Arthur defiantly, "it does."

Arthur rode to Leodegrance's castle at once to propose to Guinevere, and the lovely princess accepted without hesitation. Her father was overjoyed at the prospect of having the King of Logres as a son-in-law, so Arthur announced their wedding plans immediately. All the knights and ladies in the kingdom were invited to the celebrations. After the wedding, they lined up across the courtyard at Camelot to welcome the king and his new bride home. A rousing fanfare sounded, and the massive doors of the hall swung open slowly to reveal Merlin, who was standing in front of the most enormous round table.

"Welcome, royal King and Queen of Logres," said the sorcerer. "What you see before you is your wedding present from King Leodegrance. It has been in his family for many generations, but it is your rightful inheritance. Use it wisely."

Arthur and Guinevere gazed in awe at the extraordinary spectacle. The guests crowded in behind them in silent amazement. Spread out on the colossal table was an elaborate meal: huge raised pies and whole roasted swans, peacocks, woodcocks, pheasants and quails, great slabs of venison, succulent wild boar, pasties and puddings and mustard and mead, vast jugs of ale and ruby-red wine, lampreys and eels and spit-roasted ox, frumenty, dumplings, sweet cherry pies, all laid out together as a feast for their eyes.

But the banquet seemed almost insignificant compared with the table itself. Around the immense table there was space for dozens of people to sit comfortably. The finely polished oak surface was inlaid with intricate coats of arms. Each of the table's twenty legs was as thick as a tree trunk, carved with beautiful birds and animals and intertwined leaves and flowers. Every one of the golden seats was upholstered with the finest tapestry.

The king and queen walked majestically around the huge table, running their hands over the glistening wood, admiring the marquetry and inspecting the seats one by one. On the back of each seat was inscribed a name: Sir Balan, Sir Kay, Sir Uriens, Sir Uwain, Sir Balyn, Sir Melligrance, Sir Agravain, Sir Pellinore, Sir Launfal, Sir Bedivere, names well known to Arthur; Sir Percival, Sir Lancelot, names he did not even recognize; Sir Gawain and Sir Tor, squires who were not yet knights, and many more besides.

"When a knight dies, or is killed in battle, his name shall slowly fade and disappear," explained Merlin, "until a new knight comes to replace him."

"Well, I think my name looks quite healthy at the moment," the king joked, passing his own seat, which

41

was the grandest of all.

"Who is this one for?" he asked, stopping at an unmarked seat decorated with a huge stag.

"That is the Siege Perilous, or the dangerous seat," answered Merlin. "It is reserved for the best knight in the world. Anyone who tries to sit there will be burned to ashes, except, of course, its true and rightful occupant."

At that moment Sir Pellinore, Arthur's old enemy, strode in through the door, followed by his son, Tor.

"At your humble service, my king," they both said, to Arthur's astonishment, bowing deeply before taking their places at the table.

When everyone was seated, Arthur summoned Tor, along with his own nephew, Gawain, to be knighted. Then he and Guinevere found their own seats and looked around at the familiar smiling faces. Only the places for Sir Lancelot and Sir Percival and the Siege Perilous were empty.

Arthur banged on the table to get everyone's attention.

"No more arguments about who sits where," he announced. "All shall be equal at this table. No single knight is more important than another. From today, you shall all be known as the Knights of the Round Table, the bravest and most noble knights in the world. Your fame will spread across the kingdom and across the seas to lands far away. Stories of your adventures will be passed from one generation to the next, down the centuries. Now, raise your goblets and let us drink to the future."

"To the future!" cried the knights, holding their wine goblets high in the air.

"To King Arthur and Queen Guinevere!" called out Sir Pellinore.

"And to all the Knights of the Round Table!" added Merlin.

Everyone joined in the toast, and drank deeply to their king and their fellow knights. Then the babble of excited voices echoed around the hall and out across the courtyard as the celebrations began.

Exactly one year and many adventures later, the knights were once more gathered around the table when a trumpet sounded in the courtyard. Into the hall rode the Lady of the Lake, followed by three young squires. The tallest of them had flowing golden hair, broad shoulders and a warm, winning smile.

"I have come on Merlin's orders," said the Lady, in her lilting voice, "to present to you Lancelot du Lake, my foster son. I have brought him up in my palace in Lake Avalon. When I gave you Excalibur, you promised that you would do whatever I asked sometime in the future. Well, now that time has come. I entrust Lancelot to you. I ask that you make him a Knight of the Round Table."

Queen Guinevere's face had turned as white as a sheet. She stared at the handsome young newcomer, as if awestruck. Not noticing, King Arthur stepped forward graciously to greet him.

"Welcome to Camelot, Lancelot," said Arthur. "Your place awaits you at the table, but who are these other squires?"

"Hector and Lionel," said the Lady of the Lake. "Their seats are ready too."

Arthur turned back to face the table. In the year since his wedding celebrations, two of his knights had died. The names "SIR LIONEL" and "SIR HECTOR" were rapidly forming on the backs of the empty seats. Arthur drew his sword and gestured to the three squires to kneel before him. Lancelot was last to be knighted.

"Arise, Sir Lancelot du Lake," said Arthur. Lancelot got to his feet, strode over to Guinevere and bowed deeply, before taking his place at the table. His brown eyes twinkled in the candlelight. His broad, warm smile revealed flashing white teeth. Guinevere smiled back.

"Greetings, good knight," she said breathlessly, scarcely able to conceal the tremble in her voice.

From that day on, Lancelot vowed to serve and protect Queen Guinevere. Over the years, he won more tournaments and battles, and survived more dangerous quests, than any other knight in the kingdom, and soon he became Arthur's closest friend and most trusted ally. But his love for Guinevere grew stronger and stronger. Not one of the clever and charming princesses or beautiful young women that he met on his travels meant anything to him. Queen Guinevere was his only true love.

Sir Percival came to Camelot a few years later, by a very different route. He was brought up in the forests of Wales, never knowing his father. In fact, apart from his mother, he knew no one except animals, birds, trees, the wind and the water until the age of sixteen.

One day, he was wandering alone in the forest as usual, when five knights came riding by. Their armor sparkled in the sunshine and their bridles jingled as they trotted through the trees.

"Good morning, young man," said Lancelot when he saw the boy.

Percival was dumbstruck. He had never seen such a sight.

"Don't look so amazed," laughed another of the knights. "We won't bite!"

"Are you angels?" ventured the wide-eyed Percival, trembling with nervousness. "My mother's told me about angels," he added.

"Mere mortals, I'm afraid," laughed the knight, "on our way to Camelot."

"We're Knights of the Round Table," explained Sir

Lancelot kindly. "We serve King Arthur of Logres."

"Perhaps you could be a knight too, one day," said one of the other knights.

"But how do I do that?" asked Percival eagerly.

"By proving yourself worthy," said the knight. Then they cantered off through the forest.

This chance encounter was enough to stir Percival to action. He went straight home and told his mother that the next day he was going away to Camelot to become a Knight of the Round Table. His mother sighed deeply and cried a little, but she did not try to stop him. Merlin had already warned her that this was her son's destiny. She also knew that Percival's father, Sir Pellinore, was now a famous knight. Their son had obviously inherited his father's taste for adventure.

Percival was true to his word. Barefoot, dressed in animal skins and armed only with a hunting knife, he set off the very next day. He trudged through the forest, sleeping among gnarled tree roots, drinking from streams and eating only nuts and berries, until he came to the great white road that led to Camelot. By the time he reached the castle, his feet were raw and his legs were aching, but he did not waver from his task for the slightest moment.

By mingling with a group of servants, he managed to sneak in through the castle gates. Then he made his way towards the great hall, where the knights were eating their supper. As he stood nervously in the shadows, he saw a large man dressed in golden armor stride in through the door, snatch the golden goblet that King Arthur was drinking from, and march out into the night.

Arthur was furious. The knights clamored to be allowed to retrieve the cup, but the king would hear none of it.

"This is a trifling matter," he said, "not a quest worthy of a Knight of the Round Table. It's only a cup, after all. Some squire should go. If he can get the cup back, and returns wearing the golden armor, I'll reward him by making him a knight."

Percival saw his chance.

"I'll go!" he cried, jumping out of the shadows. All eyes turned towards the strange, scruffy youth.

"I'll fetch your cup, and I'll get the armor as well," Percival went on. "I'll be needing some anyway."

"Hah!" scoffed Sir Kay rudely. "How could a pathetic swineherd like you challenge a knight! Look at you, you're not even strong enough to wear his armor, let alone fight for it."

"What's your name, young man?" asked Arthur, ignoring his foster-brother.

"Percival, sir," came the confident answer. "And I'll get your cup, you'll see."

"You'll need a horse," said Arthur, recognizing the name from the empty seat at the table, "and a good meal too, by the looks of it, but I'll let you have a try."

So Percival was given his chance to prove himself, and Arthur was not disappointed. Three days later, the young stranger returned, looking very different from the ragged boy he had been. To everyone's amazement, Percival was dressed in the golden armor, carrying the stolen goblet and looking every inch the knight he was soon to become.

With one accurate throw of his hunting knife

through a tiny chink in the golden knight's armor, Percival had managed to fell the huge warrior and then swipe the golden goblet from his saddlebag. He had achieved his quest and proved himself worthy; his place awaited him at the Round Table.

Though Lancelot and Percival were very brave and fearless, neither was destined to occupy the Siege Perilous. For many long years the seat remained empty. Every so often, after a particularly difficult quest or very dangerous adventure, one of the knights was tempted to try sitting in it, but the moment his hand even touched one of the arm-rests, the whole seat glowed red and the knight in question would run screaming for water to soothe his burns.

"But who can it be for?" said Arthur impatiently to Merlin one day, when Lancelot had suffered just such a painful burn. "I can't imagine a knight braver than Lancelot. I think the Siege Perilous will stay empty for ever."

"Lancelot is not perfect," said Merlin, "but very soon you will know who is. Very soon indeed."

A few days later, Sir Lancelot was riding through the forest when he came across an ancient abbey. He was given a warm welcome by the nuns that lived there and led to a chamber to rest. A short while later, there was a tap on the door and in came a group of nuns leading a young man.

"This is Galahad," said the abbess. "We've looked after him since he was a baby. He's been taught by a wise man in the forest and knows how to use weapons. Now his only wish is to become a knight. We entrust him to your care."

Lancelot looked at the young man's smiling face and fair, flowing hair. There was something strangely familiar about him.

"Greetings, Galahad," said Lancelot with a smile.

"Greetings, Sir Lancelot," said the young man with a big grin.

Lancelot stayed at the old abbey for several days. He was reluctant to take Galahad back to Camelot until he had found out more about him. So every morning they did sword practice together and held mock jousts in the abbey grounds.

Lancelot was amazed at the young man's skill and speed. Several times the knight lost a sword fight or was knocked off his horse by Galahad's lance. But the younger man did not revel in his victories. He knew he still had plenty to learn and every evening he would question Lancelot about his life as a knight, or beg for stories about his quests and adventures.

Lancelot quickly grew fond of Galahad and was soon firmly convinced that he would make an excellent knight. In fact, he was secretly even a little envious of the young man's incredible skill and easy charm. It was time to return to Camelot and introduce him to King Arthur.

On the strength of Lancelot's recommendation, Arthur agreed to knight the young man and immediately summoned all the knights for the ceremony. As Galahad knelt down to be knighted, a bolt of lightning illuminated the hall. A deafening clap of thunder then shook the castle to its foundations the very second that Excalibur touched his shoulder.

"Arise, Sir Galahad, Knight of the Round Table," said Arthur.

Sir Galahad stood up and marched confidently over to the Round Table. Without a moment's hesitation, he went straight to the Siege Perilous. Ignoring the warning shouts and gasps of amazement from the other knights, he grasped the arm rests and slowly lowered himself into the seat. A breathless hush spread through the great hall, but no harm came to him.

All eyes were glued on the Siege Perilous as an inscription began to form on the back:

This is the seat of
Sir Galahad,
the best knight in the World.

The door of the great hall creaked slowly open. In the doorway stood Merlin, framed against the angry sky with his great cloak billowing out in the stormy evening air. He raised his long wooden staff and struck it three times on the floor.

"Greetings, good knights," he roared. "Welcome Sir Galahad, Knight of the Round Table and son of Sir Lancelot du Lake."

Lancelot looked as surprised as everybody else. Only Merlin had known of the existence of his son. The sorcerer had watched over the young Galahad, just as he had watched over Arthur, Percival and Lancelot in their early years. Now, at last, was the moment he had been waiting for, when like the very last piece of a beautiful jigsaw, the true occupant of the Siege Perilous was ready to take his rightful place and the Knights of the Round Table were at last complete.

Over the years that followed, the Knights of the Round Table grew famous far and wide for their amazing adventures, brave battles and feats of cunning. With their help, Arthur was able to defend and strengthen his kingdom, defeating any attackers and invaders with ease. At long last, peace had arrived in Logres: the people were happy, the laws were kept, the land prospered, and for a time it seemed that Arthur's realm would never again be torn apart by the

terrors of war.

But although Arthur was a very wise and thoughtful king, and his knights were the strongest and bravest fighters the world had ever known, not even they could control forever the forces of evil that threatened them. Although they did not yet realize it, it was not outside the kingdom, but within its boundaries, that the worst danger lay.

One evening, after another long and delicious supper, Arthur gazed around the huge circular table with satisfaction. Almost every seat was taken, and as the king looked from one of his knights to another, his heart practically overflowed with pride and happiness to think how many wonderful followers and loyal friends he now had.

Who would have thought, he asked himself wonderingly, that after such a humble childhood he should end up like this, wealthy, powerful and content? He was even lucky enough to have an extremely beautiful wife, Arthur thought proudly to himself, and he reached for Guinevere's hand. He decided that he must always try to rule all his knights and subjects as well as they served him.

At that exact moment, the door of the great hall slowly creaked open. Once more, Merlin stood in the doorway. He struck the stone floor three times with his staff, and the chatter in the hall gradually died down. The friendly clinking of cutlery subsided, and everyone turned around in their seats to listen to what the wise wizard had to say.

"Greetings, good knights," Merlin roared, and his voice seemed to contain a hint of sadness and regret. Everyone in the hall, from the king himself to the merest servant waiting at the tables, maintained a respectful silence.

"I come to bring you encouragement and strength," Merlin went on mysteriously, "but also to warn you. Be on your guard, Knights of the Round Table. Danger can lurk around any corner. He who seems your friend may be your enemy. Do not let pride become your downfall."

Arthur felt a cold chill creep through his bones and shuddered slightly, clutching his wife's hand a little tighter. How did Merlin always seem to know what he was thinking? Just a moment ago, he had been feeling proud and complacent about his good fortune. Now he had been reminded that a good knight must never become self-satisfied, and a king, despite his power and high position, must be even more careful to guard against pride.

He was about to ask the sorcerer to explain, but

before he could do so, the heavy hall door swung closed. Merlin was gone.

The
enchanted ship

"Faster!" yelled King Arthur.

It was a fine summer's afternoon and the knights were pounding through Camelot Forest at breakneck speed, in pursuit of an enormous stag. The terrified creature was crashing through the undergrowth ahead of them, wrenching off whole branches with its antlers in a frantic bid to escape. Charging after it came the knights, spurring on their horses over logs, through mud and across streams, deeper and deeper into the dark and tangled forest.

Arthur soon found himself out in front, with Sir Uriens and Sir Accolon following close behind him. Their quarry was still well within sight when they reached the other side of the forest and galloped out into the bright sunshine. Mile after mile they rode in the hazy heat of the afternoon, up hills and across valleys, over thick hedgerows and through meadows until they reached the banks of a wide, green river. There they came to an abrupt halt. The stag had disappeared. Looking all around him, Arthur realized he had no idea where they were. The horses were dripping with sweat and panting with exhaustion.

Night was falling fast.

"We can't get back to Camelot tonight," said Arthur, dismounting. "We'll have to find somewhere to shelter." So they walked wearily along the riverbank in the twilight, leading their horses behind them.

"What's that?" said Uriens all of a sudden, pointing down the mist-covered river. Peering through the gloom, Arthur could just make out a large, dark shape in the distance. It was gliding towards them, parting the fog as it cut through the muddy, green water. The three men stood transfixed on the riverbank, gazing at the looming shape as it drifted nearer and nearer, to the sound of strange, ethereal music.

"A ship!" said Accolon, squinting in the half-light. "A beautiful ship," gasped Uriens, as the vessel sailed closer. Now they could see the ornate carvings and gold that decorated its hull. Its sails billowed gently in the warm candlelight that spilled from its cabins. Soft laughter and singing filled the air as the ship floated towards the riverbank.

"Come in, good knights," called a voice from inside, as a wooden walkway was lowered onto the bank. The tired, hungry men needed little encouragement. They immediately tethered their horses, crossed the walkway and stepped on board.

Twelve beautiful faces smiled at them when they entered the cabin. Twelve graceful pairs of hands reached out to help them pull off their mud-spattered gauntlets and boots.

"Who are you, fair ladies?" asked Uriens when they

were seated at a long table with an enormous feast spread out in front of them.

"We are the damsels of the river," sang the twelve women in unison.

"This must be magic," whispered Accolon to Arthur. "Do you think it's safe?"

"I'm not sure; it may be a trick," said Arthur. His head was spinning. The room moved in and out of focus. Accolon, too, was having trouble staying awake.

"This wine. . . it's making me feel very strange," he said, drowsily.

"I think it's. . ." The laughter and music faded as his head hit the table.

Sir Accolon woke feeling groggy, wondering where he was. Somebody was kicking him repeatedly in the leg. And someone was repeating a ridiculous rhyme in an urgent, tuneless voice:

"Get up, get up mister knight,
Get up, get up for a fight.
Get up, get up, now it's light,
Get up, get up, time to fight!"

Slowly, Accolon opened his eyes. The voice belonged to a dwarf who was turning perfect cartwheels on the grass in front of him as he chanted his rhyme over and over again. At the end of each verse he ran over and kicked Accolon.

"I don't think you'll ever be a minstrel," yawned Accolon, raising his head.

"Well, I did want to be a knight," said the dwarf, "but nobody would take me seriously and I couldn't afford the armor. In the end I had to settle for fool."

None of this made any sense to Accolon. He'd fallen asleep in a magic ship, and he had woken up in a field with a dwarf gibbering in his ear. It was all too much before breakfast.

"Where am I and what do you want?" he said bluntly, brushing grass from his legs.

"You've got to fight, mister knight, now it's light, you've got to."

"Yes all right, all right, I've got that bit, but when and where, and who?"

"Whom is the pronoun you require," said the dwarf, grinning.

"Don't be facetious and answer the question," snapped Accolon.

"Oh, very well then. Tomorrow morning, here, Sir Damas, hand-to-hand combat, usual stuff. Here's a sword and scabbard, a present from Morgan le Fay." And he thrust an exquisitely decorated sword into Accolon's hand.

"But I recognize that sword. . ." said Accolon.

"Of course you do," said the dwarf, impatiently. "Now follow me."

Sir Uriens woke up back at Camelot, next to his wife, Morgan le Fay. He was confused.

"I thought I was on a ship miles from here," he mumbled.

"It must have been a dream, my dear. Now go back to sleep," whispered Morgan.

Arthur was woken by water dripping onto his nose and trickling slowly down his neck. He then became aware that he had a terrible headache, that his throat was parched and that there was something very wrong with his arms. They wouldn't move.

Opening his eyes, he discovered why. He was chained to a wall in the darkest, dankest dungeon imaginable. His legs were clamped in irons and his armor was nowhere to be seen. But worst of all, Excalibur was gone!

"So it was a trick," he murmured, suddenly remembering the enchanted ship and the damsels of the river.

In the dim light of the dreadful dungeon his eyes began to register a gruesome spectacle. Dozens of other men were chained to the walls around him. Some were groaning, and some were so thin that they looked like little more than skin-covered skeletons.

"What am I doing here?" he asked hoarsely.

"Waiting to die," croaked the man next to him. Then, one by one, all the other prisoners related their stories. They told him that they were all captives of an evil knight called Sir Damas, who had seized his brother's castle and land after the death of their father. The brother, an honest knight by the name of Sir Ontzlake, had challenged Damas to a fight in order to settle the matter. But Damas was too cowardly to accept the challenge himself, so he was in the habit of capturing wandering knights and offering them the choice of fighting in his place, or life imprisonment.

Sir Damas was so despised that every single knight so far had chosen to be imprisoned. Some had been captives for years and years. Eighteen had already perished from starvation or disease.

"But I have to get out of this godforsaken place!" screamed Arthur, tugging desperately at his bonds.

"There is no escape," said a feeble voice from the corner.

"Except in a coffin," said his grim-faced companion.

"That's if the rats don't get you first," added another, mournfully.

<hr/>

At that moment the heavy door of the dungeon creaked open and a young, fresh-faced woman bustled in. Arthur said he thought he recognized her as one of Morgan le Fay's maids, but she denied all knowledge of the sorceress. She said she had brought a message from Sir Damas, and offered Arthur the choice of fighting for the evil knight or staying imprisoned for the rest of his life, just as the other prisoners had described.

"If I have to choose, I'd rather die fighting than starve to death in this dismal rat hole!" said Arthur, surveying once again the gloomy dungeon and its miserable occupants. Suddenly, he had an idea:

"Tell Sir Damas I'll only fight for him if all my fellow prisoners are released, whatever the outcome of the fight, and if I can have a well-wrought sword and shield and a decent suit of armor."

The maid immediately called two guards, who unchained Arthur and took him up to meet Sir Damas.

"I'll agree to your conditions," said the evil knight in a wheedling, nasal drone, "but only if you promise to fight to the death."

"I promise," said Arthur.

Meanwhile, Accolon was following the dwarf to the home of Sir Ontzlake. The dwarf chattered as they walked, running ahead every so often to turn a few cartwheels and chant a few more rhymes. He explained that Accolon was to fight Sir Damas for

Morgan le Fay. The sword would ensure that Accolon won, and then he would become king and she would be queen.

Accolon agreed to this willingly. During his time at Camelot he and Morgan le Fay had fallen in love, even though she was married to Sir Uriens. Accolon didn't know exactly what the sorceress was planning, but this chance to please her was too good to miss.

When they at last arrived, Sir Ontzlake was outside to greet them.

"Welcome to my humble abode," he said, hobbling towards them. "You've arrived in good time."

"For what?" asked Accolon.

"For the fight," said Ontzlake. "You see, I've just heard that my lily-livered brother, Sir Damas, has at last agreed to settle our differences in the traditional way: hand-to-hand combat at dawn. But as you can see, I'm in no state to fight, wounded in both thighs, as luck would have it."

"So I'm here in order to fight this battle instead of you?" said Accolon.

"You are indeed," replied Ontzlake, "but if you wear my white armor and ride my horse, nobody will know the difference. Damas is a coward, and a terrible fighter. You should have no problem killing him, especially with that fine sword."

"Killing him?"

"It's a fight to the death," said Ontzlake. "Didn't I mention that?"

"To the death," repeated Accolon slowly. The dwarf chuckled and ran off across the meadows.

Very early the next morning, before it was even light, Arthur heard a knock on the door of the chamber where he had been trying to sleep. In fact, he had spent most of the night lying awake worrying about how he was going to kill Sir Ontzlake without his magic sword.

"Come in," he called.

The maid who had come to the dungeon the day before stepped into the room and thrust a package into his hands.

"Morgan le Fay sends you this with her love," the maid said, and scuttled out. Arthur quickly unwrapped the long bundle, ripping open the strings that bound its familiar shape.

"Excalibur!" he cried, clutching the gleaming

scabbard. He'd no idea how his half-sister had retrieved the sword or smuggled it to him, but it had come just in time. With Excalibur, he would defeat Ontzlake, and the magic scabbard would ensure he lost no blood, however ferocious the fight.

He quickly put on the black armor that Sir Damas had provided, and strapped the sword to his side. Just as the sun was rising, he galloped out of the gates to do battle with Sir Ontzlake.

A large crowd had gathered to watch the long-awaited clash of the brothers. The two knights, one in black and one in white, arrived from opposite ends of the meadow, both with their visors clamped firmly down so that their faces could not be seen.

They strode purposefully towards one another and stood face to face in the middle of the field. Then each knight reached down to his side, drew his sword and raised it high in the air. The crowd gasped. The razor-sharp blades that glinted and sparkled in the sun were identical!

With a great groan that rang around the battlefield, the knights clashed their swords together and a frenzied fight to the death began. Blow was exchanged for blow, strike for strike, and yell for yell as they battled through the morning. To Arthur's surprise, each blow from the white knight's sword pierced his armor and cut his flesh. But each strike from his own blade failed to have an effect.

The spectators gasped and cheered. Rarely had they seen such a splendidly savage duel. Sir Damas, far from being a coward, as they had been led to believe, was in fact extraordinarily brave. He continued to fight on with a useless sword and a badly damaged suit of armor, while his brother brought blow after blow raining down on his head.

Unaware of the roar of the crowd, and dizzy with pain, Arthur suddenly staggered backwards and fell to his knees. He lowered his head and saw blood gushing from his wounds onto the grass. He knew that something was very badly wrong.

Why was the magic scabbard not protecting him? And what had happened to Excalibur?

His opponent was now towering over him, about to deliver another blow that would probably be the last. Clenching his teeth and screaming with agony, Arthur summoned just enough strength to raise his sword to deflect the blow. As the two swords clashed again, he felt his own blade shatter into smithereens.

This was not Excalibur! Before his opponent could strike again, he had cast what was left of the weapon to the ground in fury, and struggled to his feet.

"Surrender, Sir Damas," taunted the white knight, "surrender or die!"

"I'll fight to the death," growled Arthur. Then he lowered his head, raised his shield and charged at the knight, ramming his whole weight into his opponent's stomach and knocking him over.

The white knight's sword flew from his hand as he fell sprawling on the grass. Arthur grabbed it. The moment his hand touched the handle, he knew it was the real Excalibur. His eyes darted over to the scabbard, still hanging at the white knight's side. He wrenched it off and flung it far from the fight. Now neither of them would have its protection.

"Now it's your turn for a taste of Excalibur," he shouted. He tore off the white knight's helmet, raised Excalibur and struck as hard as he could. Then he looked down. In an instant he recognized the blood-covered face that stared up at him.

"Sir Accolon!" he cried and ripped off his own helmet.

"King Arthur?" whispered Accolon.

"So you stole Excalibur!"

"No!" moaned Accolon, grimacing with pain. "It was Morgan le Fay. I promise. She sent it to me. . . after her damsels put us to sleep on the ship." Accolon was fighting for breath. "She said I should fight for her. . . but I didn't know I had to fight you. I thought you were Sir Damas."

"And I thought you were Ontzlake," said Arthur, kneeling beside him. "She tricked both of us. She put me in Damas's dungeon until I agreed to fight. . . and sent me a fake Excalibur. I trusted her, but she wanted me dead."

Arthur vowed that he would get his revenge on Morgan le Fay. Little did he know that, even as they spoke, she was carrying out the next stage of her evil plot at Camelot.

The scheming sorceress

Morgan le Fay was woken by bright sunshine streaming through a crack in the curtains and onto her face. Sir Uriens was snoring peacefully beside her.

"Still dead to the world, dear?" she whispered. "Good."

Taking care not to disturb him, she eased herself out of the bed, crept across the chamber and out of the door. It was still very early. Apart from a few maids, no one at Camelot was awake. She had plenty of time.

She slipped down the winding stairway, laughing to herself as she thought about how easy it had been to trick Arthur and get hold of Excalibur. And very soon he would be dead, killed by his own sword. Then, with the king gone and Excalibur in her grasp, she could make herself queen and marry her beloved Sir Accolon. But there was one small detail left to take care of: her husband.

"Good morning, my lady."

The maid's cheerful voice startled her.

"Oh. . . er, good morning, Alice dear," said Morgan. "I was just on my way to find you. Could you pop over to the armory and bring me a sword? It's such a lovely morning, I thought I'd do a little sword practice before breakfast."

"Er. . . yes, of course, my lady," said Alice, somewhat surprised. Her mistress seldom woke so early, nor spoke to her so politely. Nor did she usually show any interest in swords.

Alice scuttled off to the armory, fetched the sword and delivered it to Morgan, but something about her mistress's behavior was still very worrying. Was it her agitation, her oddly exaggerated gestures when she took hold of the weapon, or the strange, almost sinister, glint in her eye? Alice began to suspect the worst. Her mistress was obviously about to kill herself, and she had to do something to stop her.

At that moment, the maid found herself right outside Sir Uwain's chamber. He would know why his mother was acting so strangely. Without even stopping to knock, Alice burst in. Sir Uwain had just woken up.

"Sir, sir, I'm sorry," she gabbled frantically, "I'm worried about my lady. . . She asked for a sword, and then she said she wanted to practice, but she's heading for the staircase, and I just thought. . ."

Before Alice could even finish her sentence, Uwain had jumped out of bed. He raced along the passage to his parents' chamber, where his father was still sleeping, and hid behind the heavy curtains. Seconds later, he heard the door open. Peeking from his hiding place, he saw his mother sneak in. She tiptoed over to the bed, lifted the sword up over her husband's head, and was just about to strike when Uwain leaped out and grabbed her arms from behind.

"You wicked woman," he snarled. "How could you do this? If you weren't my own mother, I'd kill you now."

"Please, please don't tell anyone, Uwain," begged Morgan in an urgent whisper. "I can't imagine what came over me. I must have been sleepwalking. This won't happen again for as long as I live...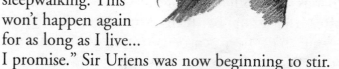

I promise." Sir Uriens was now beginning to stir.

"What's all the noise about?" he asked sleepily.

"Nothing, my dear," said Morgan sweetly. "We were just saying how peaceful you look when you're asleep." And she hurried out of the room, followed by Uwain.

"I beg you not to tell anyone," she said again, clutching desperately at her son's sleeve. "For the sake of our family, nobody must know."

Uwain was silent. He just stared at his mother with a shocked look on his face.

"Your story's very hard to believe," he said at last, "but I'll keep it a secret, for the sake of the family. And it must never happen again."

"It won't," said Morgan. "I promise."

Later that morning, a covered cart arrived at Camelot with a message for Morgan le Fay:

> *Excalibur is back with its*
> *rightful owner. Your plot*
> *has been discovered. Here*
> *is a gift from King Arthur*
> *to his sister, with his love.*

Morgan gingerly lifted the cover and peeked inside. Then she let out a loud wail and covered her face with her hands. It was the body of Sir Accolon.

After the fight between Accolon and Arthur, the king had been carried to an abbey in the middle of the forest, where his wounds were treated by a skilful surgeon. It had been too late to save Sir Accolon. He had taken his last breath on the battlefield soon after his true identity had been revealed. Arthur dispatched his body back to Camelot for burial, together with the message for his half-sister.

Before taking leave of the battlefield himself, the king had ensured that the quarrel between Damas and Ontzlake was finally settled. He ordered Damas to hand over the castle and lands to his brother, and release all the imprisoned knights. Sir Ontzlake and the knights were overjoyed at this outcome and pledged their allegiance to Arthur.

Sir Damas protested feebly, but he was far too cowardly to take any action.

When Morgan le Fay received Arthur's message, she wasted no time. She had to get Excalibur back before her brother could take his revenge. But first she had to find out where he was. Taking care to hide her grief and anger, she went straight to Queen Guinevere and asked in her sweetest voice if she could possibly visit Arthur.

"Of course," said Guinevere, knowing nothing of Morgan's trickery. "He's resting in the old abbey in the middle of the forest."

Morgan set off at once with an escort of men. She rode all night and reached the abbey at noon the following day.

"I'm King Arthur's sister," she said to the abbess on arrival. "I've come to see my poor, wounded brother."

"He's sleeping for the first time in three days," said the abbess. "Can you wait a little longer before you disturb him?"

"I just want to see him. I promise I won't wake him," Morgan replied.

The abbess led her to Arthur's room.

"You may leave us alone," said the sorceress. "I only want to watch over him for a while."

As soon as the abbess had left, Morgan crept over to the bed. Arthur was sound asleep, clutching Excalibur tightly by the blade. She didn't dare try to take it, in case he woke up. Instead, she started to ferret around the room, looking for the magic scabbard. Finally, she saw it poking out from underneath Arthur's pillow. She placed her fingers carefully around the end and began to ease the scabbard out, very, very slowly. Just then, Arthur murmured and rolled over.

"Blast!" she cursed under her breath. Her hand was trapped under Arthur's head! She muttered a quick spell to ensure it was Guinevere's voice that Arthur heard and Guinevere's soft hand he felt patting his shoulder.

"Move over, my darling, you've fallen asleep on my hand," Morgan whispered. Arthur mumbled a sleepy apology and rolled over in the bed. Morgan le Fay whipped the scabbard out from under the pillow and hurried out. When she rode away from the abbey, nobody knew the scabbard was hidden under her cloak.

Arthur was furious when he woke up to discover that Morgan had visited the abbey while he slept, and that the magic scabbard was gone. He set off at once in pursuit of his sister, stopping for Sir Ontzlake on the way. They had not ridden far when they met a shepherd on the road.

"Have you seen a woman with jet black hair, riding with a group of armed men?" Arthur asked the man.

"They galloped past just a couple of minutes

ago, sir," said the shepherd. "Fast as the wind, they were. Scattered my sheep everywhere, and. . ."

Without even stopping to thank the man, Arthur and Ontzlake shot off in the direction he had indicated. Before long, they caught sight of the wicked sorceress in the distance, galloping along the shore of Lake Avalon at the head of her entourage. They were still too far away to see her take the scabbard from beneath her swirling cloak.

"If I can't have it, then nobody can," Morgan le Fay sneered, launching the scabbard high into the air. It soared across the sky and then plunged into the middle of the lake with a loud splash, sinking without a trace.

Morgan hurtled on along the shore. Arthur and Ontzlake charged after her, up the mountainside, around a huge rock and into a steep-sided valley. There they came to a sudden halt. Morgan le Fay had vanished!

"Where on earth is she?" wailed Arthur, looking wildly around. All he could see were scores of strangely shaped boulders in the valley below. Confused and exhausted, the two knights gave up and set off dejectedly back towards Camelot. The moment they were out of sight, one of the boulders let out a loud cackle and began to change back into human form. It was Morgan le Fay. As her spell wore off, the other rocks melted back into men on horseback.

Queen Guinevere was elated at her husband's safe return, and organized an elaborate feast in his honor. Arthur, though still weak and tired from his long ordeal, summoned just enough energy to tell the Knights of the Round Table all about his adventures. The knights were outraged when they heard about Morgan le Fay's evil plot to kill their king, and many swore to seek revenge.

Six days later, when Arthur had fully recovered, a maid arrived at Camelot saying that she had a gift for the king. She was shown into the great hall.

"Your sister sends you this as a peace offering, in the hope that you will find it in your heart to forgive her," the maid said, as she thrust towards him the most spectacular and expensive-looking cloak Arthur had ever seen.

"It's marvelous!" exclaimed the queen. "What a

magnificent present. You should try it on at once."

Arthur reached out, and was just about to take the cloak, when he suddenly had an idea.

"Let me see it on you first," he said to the maid.

"Oh no, no, sir, I couldn't possibly wear this," she gabbled nervously. "This cloak is for someone else entirely. I mean, this cloak is meant for a king."

"But I insist," said Arthur, beckoning to two of his knights. "Come on. We'll help you put it on."

The two knights gently took the heavy cloak from the flustered young woman and placed it around her shoulders. Then they leaped back in surprise and amazement, as the maid burst into flames! In an instant, she was no more than a pile of smoldering ashes on the floor.

The great hall fell silent. All eyes turned towards Arthur.

"That evil, cowardly, vicious, scheming serpent!" he hissed, almost purple with rage. "So this is her idea of a peace offering. I've had enough of her trickery and her lies." He glanced around the hall to make sure that everybody was listening as he raised his voice to a thunderous roar that rattled the rafters and could be heard deep in the darkest dungeons of Camelot.

"Bear witness to my words, good knights. Morgan le Fay is no sister of mine! From this day on she is banished from my heart, my court and my kingdom."

Then, with his words still echoing around the room

and the pile of ashes still smoldering on the cold, stone floor, he strode straight across the great hall and out through the door.

"Forever!" he shouted at the top of his voice, before slamming the heavy, wooden door behind him.

Sir Gawain and the Green Knight

"Silence!" shouted Sir Gawain one New Year's Day, banging his goblet on the Round Table. The whole court had gathered in the great hall at Camelot, and the first course of a huge feast had just been carried in to the sound of a trumpet fanfare.

"Silence for the king," Sir Gawain yelled once more. The music faded, the babble of voices died down and soon only the crackling of the log fires broke the silence.

"Thank you, ladies and gentlemen," said Arthur. "Now, before we begin this splendid feast, what spectacle or adventure awaits us?" It was a custom at Camelot that on feast days the king would not start eating until he had seen a brave deed or a strange marvel, or heard a tale of a dangerous quest.

"Come on, Knights of the Round . . ."

A loud commotion out in the courtyard and the clatter of horseshoes on stone cut him off in mid sentence. The massive doors of the hall flew open, and in rode an enormous man on an enormous horse. He was far taller than any ordinary man, with huge hands, large, powerful limbs and piercing, red eyes set in a fierce face. But the most extraordinary thing about him, which made everyone gape in amazement, was that he was bright green all over.

Not only were his clothes green, but his hands were green and his face was green. His long, thick hair and the big, shaggy beard that spread all over his chest were as green as grass. Even his gigantic horse was green from head to hoof. He carried no weapons except a colossal, green battle-ax clasped in one hand. The other hand held a big branch of holly high above his head.

The Green Knight rode proudly through the stunned silence of the hall, surveying the scene. Then he cast the holly down on the floor and called out: "Who's in charge here?" His big, booming voice echoed around the cavernous hall. No one answered. Like everyone else, Arthur was dumbstruck. He stared at the bright green figure in total astonishment. Several moments elapsed before he had recovered enough to greet the stranger and invite him to the feast.

"I haven't come to eat with you," said the Green Knight bluntly, "and don't worry, I'm not here for a fight, either. That's why I brought a branch instead of a sword, and if I wanted a fight, I'd be wearing my armor, wouldn't I?" Arthur breathed a quiet sigh of relief; the prospect of having to get up to fight this huge man instead of sitting down for a feast was not one he relished.

"What I can offer you," the knight went on, swinging his ax casually, "is a little New Year's challenge. The fame of your knights has spread, you see. We've even heard about their brave deeds in my castle in the north, so I've come to set them a small test to find out if their reputation is deserved."

"Sir," replied the king, "I'm sure there are plenty of people here who would joust with you, or fight in single combat, if that's what you have in mind."

"No!" boomed the knight. "I've told you, I don't want to fight. These boys would have no chance against me, anyway. They're far too feeble." He was staring directly at Gawain. A wave of anger swept around the table, but nobody dared to respond.

"But if anyone here is brave enough to exchange just one blow for another," he said, "I'll hand over my ax and let him strike me first. He can aim the blow wherever he wants, and I promise I won't even flinch, as long as I can return the blow exactly a year from today."

At this point, the Green Knight rolled his red eyes ferociously, brandished his ax and looked all around the hall for someone to answer his challenge. When nobody stepped forward, he roared with laughter.

"Is this really the great court of King Arthur?" roared the knight scornfully. "And can these really be the famous Knights of the Round Table? I don't know how you earned your reputation, when just the mention of an ax makes you all tremble with fear!" Then he rocked with laughter again, until Arthur's face went red with embarrassment. But his shame soon turned into anger, and unable to bear the gibes a moment longer, he sprang forward.

"This is madness, sir!" he said, striding over to face the huge man. "But if you really want to play such a stupid game, give me your ax and get ready!" The Green Knight dismounted and handed the heavy weapon to Arthur. The king gripped its huge handle, and was preparing to strike when Sir Gawain jumped up from his seat.

"Please, Uncle," he said, "let me accept instead of you. I've yet to prove myself worthy as a Knight of the Round Table, and this could be my chance."

At first Arthur was reluctant to let Gawain take his place, but he was swayed by the eager expression on the young man's face, so he handed him the ax and wished him luck.

"I'm glad that at least one of you so-called knights is brave enough to accept," said the Green Knight. "What's your name, boy?"

"My name is Gawain," came the answer, "and I'm a Knight of the Round Table, not a boy. And as a knight I give you my promise that I will strike one blow, on the understanding that whatever happens, you will return the blow a year from today."

"I'm pleased you accept the terms of the agreement," said the knight. "After you've struck your blow, I'll tell you who I am and how to find me in a year's time. But now, let's see what you can do with the ax. You have just one try. Do your worst."

The knight then knelt down on the floor, bowed his head and pulled his long hair forward to expose the back of his green neck. Gawain gripped the ax firmly, took a deep breath, and with all his strength swung it high into the air. Then, taking a small step forward, he brought it swiftly down on the knight's bare neck with such great force that the  razor-sharp blade sliced straight through the flesh and bone, and sent sparks flying as it hit the cold, stone floor.

The huge head thudded to the ground and rolled across the floor. Blood spurted from the severed neck, bright red against the green, but the knight did not falter or fall. He stood up and strode forward, grabbed his head by the hair and, turning to his horse, swung himself into the saddle as if nothing unusual had happened.

Amidst gasps of astonishment, he raised his head in his hand and turned its face towards Gawain. Out of the mouth came these words:

"Keep your promise, Sir Gawain,
To meet me next New Year's Day.
It will not be hard to track me down,
Though my castle is far away.

Through the mountains and valleys of Wales,
To the Forest of Wirral beyond,
At the place called the Green Chapel,
There we will seal our bond.

Ask for the knight of that chapel,
For many there know me by name.
If you search me out, you shall find me.
If you fail, you shall live in shame."

And with that, the Knight of the Green Chapel spurred his horse to a gallop and clattered out of the doors, across the courtyard and away into the night through the swirling snow, still dangling his head by its long, green hair.

The year passed quickly for Gawain, as season followed season. The New Year celebrations came to an end, the snow melted and fresh green leaves appeared on the trees. The chill winds of spring gave way to summer's heat, and the sweet, rich scent of roses faded all too quickly when the meadows were filled with the cries of reapers. At last, when the harvest had been gathered in and the woodpiles were stacked high, Gawain began to prepare for his quest to meet the Green Knight.

On the first morning of November, he strapped on his armor and sword, and with the Green Knight's ax in his hand, mounted his horse, Gringalet. His squire handed him his helmet. Then, remembering the knight's words, Gawain set off on his mysterious quest, riding alone through the Kingdom of Logres to the wild mountains and deep, wooded valleys of Wales, through driving rain and snow, across icy rivers shrouded in fog, through deep, dark forests and along lonely, windswept clifftops.

At night, he slept in his armor among the cold, craggy rocks, fearful of attack from wolves, bears and robbers. By day, he pressed onwards, fighting long and bloody battles with the dragons, monsters and giants which in those days still lived in the wilderness. Few others could have survived all the dangers and hardships of that bitter winter, but Gawain struggled on until he reached the Forest of Wirral. He asked everyone he met if they knew the Knight of the Green Chapel, but no one had even heard of him.

On Christmas Eve, disheartened, cold and weary, Gawain prayed he might find somewhere to shelter. All of a sudden, the swirling mists parted, the marshland gave way to parkland, and in the distance he caught sight of a magnificent castle.

"Thank God," thought Gawain. "Now I can only pray that whoever lives there will welcome me in for Christmas."

His prayers were answered soon enough, for he was met with a warm welcome when he knocked on the imposing gate. The moment he entered the grand courtyard, servants and squires scurried around to help him dismount. Gringalet was led away to the stables for food, water and rest, and the grateful Gawain was shown to a hall where a big log fire burned brightly in the hearth.

The lord of the castle, a large, genial man with a bushy, red beard and thick, red hair, clasped Gawain firmly by the hand, welcomed him to his home and invited him to stay for as long as he wished. He said that everyone at the castle was delighted that a famous

Knight of the Round Table had found his way to such a remote place.

Gawain was treated with the utmost hospitality. The squires took him to a chamber, helped him remove his rusty armor and gave him soft, fur-lined robes to wear. Then they led him back to a comfortable chair near the fire, where a sumptuous feast awaited him.

After the meal, the lady of the castle came in. She was one of the most beautiful women Gawain had ever seen in his life. Gawain spoke to her very politely, bowing deeply and kissing her hand, smiling, laughing and taking every opportunity to display the skills in conversation and courtly manners for which he was justly renowned.

On Christmas Day, many more guests arrived, and three whole days passed quickly in feasting and celebration. Gawain enjoyed himself so much that he almost forgot why he was there. At each meal he found the lady sitting next to him, always chattering, giggling and ordering her servants to attend to him.

On the fourth day, most of the guests left early. But when Gawain began to get ready to go, the lord stopped him.

"Must you leave us so soon?" he asked. "Please stay a little longer, unless you think we're unworthy to have such a noble guest."

"It's certainly not that," said Gawain. "You've been

extremely generous, but I must leave to find the Green Chapel. I made a promise that I'd be there on New Year's Day, and I don't even know where it is yet."

"Then we're all in luck," said the lord. "The Green Chapel is only a few miles from here, so you can stay with us until the day of your appointment. We'd be delighted to have you." Gawain was relieved to hear this, and tried to put all thoughts of the Green Knight out of his mind as he agreed to stay.

"I'm sure you're still tired from your journey," said the lord. "What you need is rest and plenty to eat before you go. Why don't you have a lie-in tomorrow and come down when you feel like it? I'm going to be out in the forest all day, hunting deer, but my wife can look after you." Gawain said he thought this was a good idea.

"And let's make a bargain," added the lord, "that in the evening we'll swap whatever we've won during the day." Gawain agreed to play this game, even though he didn't really know what the lord meant.

The next morning, when the lord left, Gawain dozed in his bed, protected from drafts by the thick curtains which hung all around it. He was woken by a tapping on the door, and peeking out from behind the curtains, he saw the lady of the castle poking her head into the room.

"Good morning, Sir Gawain," she said sweetly. "It's time to wake up. It would be a shame to spend the morning in bed, when we've so much to talk about." Then she closed the door gently. Gawain was still sleepy and didn't feel like leaving his warm bed. But he didn't want to be rude, so he got up, dressed and went downstairs.

"Here's my favorite knight, at last," giggled the lady when she saw him. "And as my husband's away, I can do exactly what I want with you." She straightened his tunic and brushed imaginary specks from his shoulders. Then she sat down at the table and patted the space next to her. "Now come and sit beside me and we'll have a little chat."

And so she went on, talking, laughing and flirting all morning. Gawain responded courteously but coolly, pretending that he didn't understand what she was hinting at. Although she was extremely beautiful, he knew she was his host's wife, and that he was a Knight of the Round Table. And in truth he was not really in the mood for games like these, as the shadow of his meeting with the Green Knight loomed ever closer.

When the lady finally got up to leave the room,

Gawain made no attempt to stop her. She looked at him slightly disdainfully and said: "It's hard to believe that you're really Sir Gawain."

"And why's that?" he asked anxiously, worried that he had offended her.

"Because Sir Gawain would never spend such a long time with a lady and then let her leave without asking for a kiss."

"If that is your wish, I will comply," he replied. She leaned forward gracefully and kissed him, then got up and left.

When the lord came home with the deer he had killed that day, he offered them to Gawain in exchange for whatever he had won. In return, Gawain put his hands around the lord's neck and kissed him.

"Is that what you won today?" asked the lord, looking rather surprised.

"That's all," said Gawain, "and I give it to you freely, just as it was given to me."

"But where did you get it from?" asked the lord.

"Telling you that was not part of our agreement," said Gawain, and they both laughed. On the way to supper they agreed that they would play the same game the following day.

The next morning, the lord left early to hunt wild boar in the marshes. After he'd left, the lady spent all morning trying to seduce Gawain. But once again he resisted her advances by turning them into a joke, though with such skill that he managed not to offend her. By the end of the morning, all that she had given him were two kisses.

When the lord returned, he presented Gawain with a huge wild boar and, without explanation, Gawain gave him two kisses.

"You have done well," laughed the lord, as they went to supper.

All evening the lady flirted with Gawain, right under her husband's nose, and all evening Gawain treated her very politely. At last, the lord announced that the next day he was going to hunt foxes, and suggested that they should renew their bargain. Gawain agreed. The next morning, when the lord left at sunrise, he lay in bed, having nightmares about the Green Knight.

Gawain was woken by sunshine streaming into the room as the lady threw open the window to let in the frosty morning air.

"Still asleep, Sir Gawain?" she asked. "And on such a fine morning. What a lazy knight you are today!"

When he came down, she kissed him good morning. She looked astonishingly beautiful in her long robe and green sash, her lustrous hair decorated with sparkling jewels. They chatted all morning, and she flirted even more than usual. Gawain trod a perilous path. If he rejected her, he might offend her, yet if he responded in the way she wanted, he'd be betraying his host. So, cleverly, he kept avoiding the subject, and tactfully fended off her declarations of love.

"Your heart must be made of ice," she said at last. "Why do I only get one kiss? You must have another lady at Camelot."

"No other lady has my love, but I cannot love you, even though you are so lovely," he replied, "for you already have a husband who's a better man than me."

"But just for today we could forget that, couldn't we?" she asked.

"I'm afraid not," he replied. "Because I am a knight, and I would bring shame upon my knighthood if I forgot that even for a moment."

"You may be a virtuous knight, but I'll have to spend the rest of my life in mourning," she said, sighing and kissing him sweetly. "But even if you'll accept nothing else, please at least take this sash." She unfastened the green, silk sash and offered it to Gawain, but he refused to take it.

"You're wrong if you think it's not worth much," she said, still holding out the sash. "It has magical powers. Anybody who wears it cannot be killed."

Gawain needed no more persuading. He was thinking again about the Green Knight. Something that might save his life was impossible to resist. He took the sash.

"Don't worry," said the lady, "my husband needn't

know about it. Hide it under your clothes and don't tell him." With this, she kissed him for a third time and left.

That evening, when Gawain met the lord, he said right away: "Let me be the first to give you my winnings," and kissed him three times. He didn't mention the sash.

"You've done even better than yesterday," said the lord, "and all I have to offer is a smelly fox skin."

After dinner, Gawain thanked his host and reminded him of his appointment at the Green Chapel. The lord promised to provide a guide to show him the way.

Gawain hardly slept a wink that night. He got up before it was light and put on his newly polished armor, not forgetting first to tie the sash around his waist. Then he seized his weapons, went out to the stables, mounted Gringalet and followed his guide out of the gates. It was a bitterly cold day. Snow had piled up in great drifts overnight and the freezing wind chilled the two men to the bone. They rode through driving sleet across a valley and up a wooded hillside, onto high moorland cloaked in fog. At last, the guide stopped and turned to Gawain.

"We're not far from the chapel now, sir," he said. "I'm turning back, and if I were you, I'd do the same.

That knight's an evil monster. He'll kill anyone who goes near him. Why don't you go home now? I promise I won't tell anybody. I beg you not to go down there, sir. . . you won't escape."

"I thank you for your advice," said Gawain to the terrified man, "but I am a knight and I must keep my promise. It would be cowardly to run away now." He tried to sound calm, but couldn't stop his armor rattling as he trembled with fear.

"Well, if you're so keen to die, I'm not going to stop you," said the guide. "Follow this path to the bottom of the valley. When you come to a clearing, you'll see the chapel on your left. Now goodbye and good luck. You'll need it. I wouldn't be in your shoes for all the gold in the world." Then he galloped away, as though fleeing the devil himself.

Gawain's heart was thumping wildly as he spurred Gringalet on down a winding path and into the

gloomy valley. By the time he reached the clearing he was numb with fear. On his left there was nothing that resembled a chapel, only a mound near a waterfall. He rode over, dismounted and began to walk around. Could this grass-covered hill be what he was looking for? It had several openings, and was hollow. He plucked up enough courage to poke his head inside. It was dark, dank and empty.

"What a strange place," he thought, as he climbed onto the top of the mound.

Just then, he was startled by a loud grinding noise that echoed all around the valley. It sounded like a reaper sharpening his scythe. With horror, Gawain realized it was the sound of an ax being sharpened.

"Where are you?" he yelled. There was no reply. The grinding continued.

"Show yourself, Green Knight. Let's get this over and done with."

"Wait!" boomed a voice from above. "You'll get what you've been promised, just as soon as my weapon is sharp enough."

Then, suddenly, out of a hole in the grassy mound, appeared the Green Knight, effortlessly whirling a massive, new ax above his head, which was once more firmly attached to his body. He looked even larger and fiercer than Gawain remembered.

"Welcome to my humble abode, Sir Gawain," he said. "You've arrived in good time to keep our appointment. Well, don't worry, you'll soon be repaid for your efforts. Now, off with that helmet and take what you're owed. Offer no more resistance than I did when you sliced off my head with one blow."

"Get ready to strike," said Gawain. "I'll do nothing to stop you." He knelt on the snow-covered grass, bowed his head and bared his neck, muttering a prayer under his breath. The Green Knight whirled the ax around, then raised it above his head and was just about to strike when Gawain twitched.

"The brave Sir Gawain isn't afraid of the sound of an ax, is he?" taunted the knight. "I didn't flinch before you cut off my head."

"It happened once," said Gawain, "but it won't happen again, even though I cannot replace my head, as you can. Strike away."

Once more the Green Knight whirled his ax and got ready to strike. Gawain shut his eyes, clenched his teeth and held his breath. The knight raised the ax high into the air and brought it down, missing Gawain's head by a hair's breadth, but this time Gawain didn't move a muscle, even as he heard the blade whistle past his ear.

"That's more like it," said the Green Knight. "Your courage has returned. Now pull your hood back a bit, so I can make a nice, clean cut."

"Just get on with it!" screamed Gawain suddenly. "Stop playing games. Are you afraid to kill me?"

The Green Knight swung the weapon a third time, and, with a mighty groan, brought the blade hurtling

to the ground.

Gawain took a deep breath and opened his eyes. He was still alive! Then he felt a stinging pain on the side of his neck. His fingers reached up and found a thin gash where the ax had nicked his flesh. Blood dripped onto the snow. He sprang up, seized his sword and in an instant was ready to fight.

"No more," he said. "You've had your chance. I've kept my side of the bargain, now if you try to strike me again, I'll hit back, harder than you could ever imagine."

The Green Knight stepped back and leaned on his

ax. He watched Gawain calmly for a while and then said quietly:

"I will not strike again, Sir Gawain. You're released from your bond. I could have cut off your head, but I had already tested you and found you to be true. The first blow and the second were for the one and two kisses from my wife that you gave back to me at my castle. Don't look so surprised, Sir Gawain. I know about what went on between you, because I put her up to it. Only the third time did you fail, when you gave me the kisses but not the sash that you have hidden under your armor, and for that small failing I gave you this small wound.

"You have proved to be a noble and honest knight. If you had yielded to temptation and brought shame on your knighthood, your head would now be rolling around at my feet, but you did not. Your honor is indeed true. Your only fault was love of your own life. I know that's why you took the sash, and for that I forgive you."

"Take the wretched thing!" said Gawain, pulling out the sash from under his armor. "I was a coward to accept it and a fool not to tell you about it. I've broken my promise and am not worthy to be called a knight. Kill me now. I deserve to die."

"Don't be so hard on yourself for such a small mistake," said the knight, with a laugh that Gawain knew well. "You've suffered enough. Now keep the sash and come back to my castle to celebrate."

"This time I must refuse," said Gawain, "but I'll

keep the sash as a reminder of my weakness. Now I must go home, but before I do, I beg you to tell me who you are. Where do you get your powers from? How can you turn into a green man who can survive having his head cut off?"

"My name is Sir Bercilak," the knight replied, "and it was Morgan le Fay who devised this plan. She came to my castle one day and cast a spell to turn me into the Green Knight. Then she sent me to Camelot. She also hatched the plot to see if you could resist my wife's charms. She wanted to see if Arthur's knights really do deserve their reputation for chivalry and bravery, and you, Sir Gawain, have proved beyond all doubt that they do."

For a moment, Gawain wondered why Morgan le Fay would do a thing like this; but he thanked Sir Bercilak anyway for his kind words, waved goodbye and set off. With his ordeal finally over, his only wish was to return to Camelot as quickly as possible, to see his friends and fellow knights, and let them know he was alive.

One chilly winter's afternoon, King Arthur was walking in the courtyard at Camelot when a tall, bearded knight, wearing rusty armor, came riding wearily across the drawbridge on a bony horse. Arthur noticed first a piece of tattered green silk tied around his arm and then, when the knight removed his helmet, a long, thin scar on the side of his neck.

"Greetings, noble knight. You look in need of a good rest and some sustenance," Arthur said. Sir Gawain smiled.

"King Arthur and his knights welcome you to the castle of Camelot," the king went on. "Will you tell us your name?"

"You don't recognize me, do you?" replied Gawain. "My name is Sir Gawain, and I am proud to be able to call myself a Knight of the Round Table."

Lancelot and Guinevere

Over the years, King Arthur and the Knights of the Round Table had many more adventures. There is not space here to tell of all their daring exploits, their noble quests, their acts of courage and their fierce battles, but during all this time, Lancelot and Guinevere's love for each other never waned.

Every time her handsome knight was away from Camelot, the queen grew restless. Lancelot's most perilous quest of all, the search for the Holy Grail, had taken him to distant lands for almost a year. Guinevere had waited with growing anxiety. When Lancelot finally returned, his news plunged the court into mourning: he had failed in the quest, and his son, Galahad, had died completing it. But Guinevere felt only joy at having him back again.

Now, each time Lancelot returned unharmed from his latest exploit, she found it harder and harder to conceal her delight and relief. And in the end, their friendship did not go entirely unnoticed.

Stableboys and grooms began to remark upon how often the pair went riding together. Two Knights of the Round Table, Sir Agravain and Sir Mordred, could often be seen whispering in dark corners. Cooks and maids chattered on the stairs. But any rumors that reached the king's ears were swiftly dismissed as groundless gossip, and Merlin's old warnings about Guinevere went unheeded. Until one fateful day. . .

Sir Mordred had come to court as a young squire, while Sir Lancelot had been missing. The young man's name seemed vaguely familiar to Arthur from something Merlin had once said, but the king cast any doubts aside and accepted him willingly into the fellowship of the Round Table. What Arthur did not know was that Mordred had been sent there by Morgan le Fay, to make trouble. Beneath the façade of loyal knight and trusted friend was hidden a deep and savage hatred of Arthur, and a fanatical jealousy of Lancelot.

"My day will come," said Mordred to Morgan le Fay at one of their secret meetings.

"Indeed it will," said the sorceress. "Your day will come soon."

Sir Lancelot was still one of the very best knights at Camelot, and he remained Arthur's favorite. But Lancelot knew he could never be truly noble as long as he loved the queen. He became convinced that the only way to extinguish his passion was to try to avoid her as much as possible. So he jumped at any chance to leave Camelot on a mission or quest, sometimes spending long, lonely days just riding through the forest. The queen soon noticed his frequent absences and reluctance to spend time with her.

"You've grown cold towards me," she said to him one spring day. "Have you fallen for another lady now?"

"You know I could never love another," replied Lancelot. "But you're still the wife of my best friend and king. How can I ever be a good knight when I love another man's wife? I'm just trying to avoid the pain that our meetings bring to both of us. . . and to preserve your good name. You know people are talking."

"But it's all lies!" shouted Guinevere. "You know we have nothing to be ashamed of. You're just tired of me. Well I'm tired too. I'm tired of never knowing where you are and I'm tired of waiting for you to return. How can you possibly protect me when you're hardly ever here?"

Lancelot protested that he was still her protector, but his arguments fell on deaf ears. The queen was too upset to listen and told him to leave at once. Lancelot went straight to the stables, saddled his horse and rode sadly off into the forest.

Guinevere soon bitterly regretted her angry words and wanted to apologize to Lancelot, but she couldn't. Nobody knew where he was.

The next day, when Lancelot had still not returned,

the queen decided to go riding in the woods. She did not reveal to the maids and knights who accompanied her the real reason for the outing: to look for her beloved knight.

"This is my favorite time of year," said Guinevere, as they trotted gently through a sea of bluebells in the dappled sunlight.

"Is that because it's a time for lovers?" said one of her ladies with a little giggle.

Suddenly an arrow whizzed past her ear, and Guinevere froze. Her eyes darted rapidly from one side to the other, and she realized with horror that they were surrounded by soldiers. Armed men on horseback stood poised among the trees on all sides, while scores of archers, their bows at the ready, lurked behind the bushes that grew on the forest floor.

"Do not attempt to fight us," said a voice behind her. Guinevere spun round.

It was Sir Melligrance, a Knight of the Round Table. He had long been enamored of Guinevere, but she felt nothing for him except loathing. What he couldn't get by natural appeal he had decided to take by force, and with Lancelot away and Guinevere deep in the forest, he had at last seen his chance to kidnap her.

The queen's knights did their best to defend her from Melligrance's clutches, but they were not even wearing their armor, so the battle easily went against them. Within minutes, they all lay sprawling and injured on the ground. Melligrance's men waded in through the flowers to finish them off.

"Stop!" screamed Guinevere. "Don't kill them. I'll do whatever you want, but please spare my knights and servants."

"Then come to my castle without a struggle," said Melligrance, with a wicked smirk.

As the party was led off through the forest, a brave young maid slipped away unnoticed from the back of the group and sprinted off through the trees.

Queen Guinevere looked out of the window from the high tower where she was held captive.

"Look," she said to her maid. A farmer's cart was approaching the castle at an alarming speed, swaying from side to side and nearly overturning each time it took a bend. As it drew closer to them, Guinevere let out a cry of excitement.

"It's him!"

"Who, madam?"

"Sir Lancelot, of course!" cried Guinevere delightedly.

Lancelot's sudden arrival took the castle guards by surprise, and he was inside the walls before they could start raising the drawbridge. Like an angry bull, he charged across the courtyard, impervious to the arrows of the bowmen on the ramparts. Fighting off every swordsman who crossed his path, he quickly gained access to the castle and rampaged through the narrow passageways, bellowing at the top of his voice:

"Cowardly cur! Hound from hell! Treacherous viper! Where are you, Melligrance? Come out and fight." When Melligrance recognized Lancelot's voice, he ran straight to the queen.

"Help me!" he begged. "He'll kill me."

"Why should I help you, you traitor?" said Guinevere haughtily.

"I spared your knights. Please remember that. I'll do whatever you want."

"All I want is my freedom," said Guinevere. Lancelot could now be heard at the foot of the spiral stairway leading up to the tower:

"Loathsome slug! Barbarous brute! Slimy reptile!" His insults thundered up the staircase. He was just about to storm up the steps.

Melligrance opened the door, shoved Guinevere unceremoniously out, and slammed it shut behind her. She came tumbling down the stone stairway and landed safely in Lancelot's arms. As soon as he'd made sure she was unhurt, Lancelot bounded up the last flight of steps and flung open the door. The room was empty, except for the maid cowering in the corner.

"Where is the vile toad?" he yelled.

The maid raised her eyes to the rafters and screamed as, with a great cry, Melligrance leaped onto Lancelot's back and began to tighten his arms around his neck. Quick as a flash, Lancelot reached up and grabbed the traitor's arms. Then he bent forward, flipped him over his head like a rag doll and dashed him to the floor. The defeated kidnapper lay on his back, winded and whimpering with pain. In an instant, the point of Lancelot's sword was at his throat.

"No!" croaked Melligrance.

"No!" echoed a voice in the doorway. It was Guinevere. "He spared my knights. He doesn't deserve to die."

Lancelot did not move. His eyes were wild with fury. Sweat was pouring down his face and his chest was heaving. The injured knight lay rigid and motionless on the floor, white with terror. His bulging eyes stared up at Lancelot.

"Be merciful, Lancelot," said the queen softly. Lancelot lifted his sword barely an inch.

"If you ever come anywhere near the queen again, I'll make mincemeat of you," he snarled. "Do you

109

understand me?"

"Yes," whispered Melligrance.

"How on earth did you know where to find me?" Guinevere asked Lancelot, when they were on their way back to Camelot.

"It was one of your maids," replied Lancelot. "I was riding up the hill back to Camelot, when she hurtled through a hedge onto the road in front of me. I nearly knocked her down! As soon as she'd explained what had happened, I shot off to rescue you, but my horse was felled by an archer's arrow before I could get anywhere near the castle. So I grabbed the farm cart for the final stretch."

"I knew you would come," said Guinevere with an affectionate smile. "My knight in the cart."

The story of Lancelot's daring rescue reached Camelot before he did, and he returned with Guinevere to a hero's welcome. In front of the whole court, Arthur thanked him for saving the queen from Melligrance's evil intentions.

With all the excitement, Guinevere had still not had the chance to apologize to Lancelot for her angry words, so she arranged to meet him secretly in the garden that evening. But they were not the only ones taking the air that night. Sir Mordred, spurred on by his jealousy of Lancelot, who it seemed could do no wrong in the king's eyes, had decided it was time to take action. With his accomplice, Sir Agravain, he had followed Lancelot into the garden and hidden behind a thick yew hedge to spy on the couple and listen to their words of love.

"Come and see me in my chamber tonight," they heard the queen whisper. It was exactly what they wanted to hear.

"They're traitors!" cried Mordred triumphantly, bursting into Arthur's chamber later the same night, without even bothering to knock.

"What are you talking about, Mordred?" asked Arthur calmly.

"Sir Lancelot and the queen. We caught them together in her chamber this evening. We have witnesses to prove it," crowed Mordred.

Arthur stared at Mordred long and hard before responding.

"Tell me more," he said finally. His face had hardened, but there were tears in his eyes.

"Lancelot escaped, but we've arrested the queen," said Mordred. "She's sitting in the dungeon as we speak. And you know the punishment for infidelity as well as I do. The queen must die!"

Arthur's head was lowered and his eyes downcast. A few tears splashed onto the gray stone floor. For his whole marriage, he had tried to ignore suggestions that his wife was not entirely faithful. He had pretended not to see the look in her eye when Lancelot came into view, and had told himself not to worry when both of them disappeared for hours on end. He loved Guinevere, and he was reluctant to challenge her. Nor could he bear to confront Sir Lancelot, who was his best friend and his bravest knight.

But now he could no longer deny that he had been made a fool of, and he would have to do something. If he didn't act soon, and firmly, no one would respect his leadership.

"I cannot make exceptions. . . even for my own wife," he sobbed quietly. Gulping back the tears, he drew himself up to his full height and looked Mordred in the face. "The laws of the land must be upheld. Do what has to be done."

And so it was that one gray, misty morning a few days later, Guinevere, blindfolded and dressed in a tattered, linen robe, was led out into the marketplace to be burned at the stake. A priest administered the last rites, and then the queen was hauled up onto the pyre of sticks and brushwood, and tied firmly to the stake with thick ropes. But she refused to show any shame or regret, for she knew she had done nothing wrong. Even when she smelled the acrid smoke from the torch, as it was carried solemnly across the flagstones, she held her head high.

Mordred and his armed men encircled the unlit bonfire. The other knights, unarmed and clothed in black, stood behind them with their heads bowed. Of the whole court, King Arthur alone was absent. He was spending the fateful day in his chambers, as he couldn't bear to witness the execution of his once-beloved wife. Only the heartbroken weeping of Guinevere's loyal maids broke the sorrowful silence.

As the bearer of the torch neared the center of the square, there was a stirring at the back of the crowd. The sea of bodies suddenly parted to let through a band of knights, galloping towards the queen at breakneck speed. Mordred and his crew scarcely had time to draw their swords before the knights had forced their way through to the fire, cutting down anyone who stood in their path. The leader of the group, riding a mighty stallion, leaped from his mount onto the pyre, and, using his razor-sharp sword, swiftly slashed the bonds that tied Guinevere to the stake. Then, as his men fought off any remaining opponents, he carefully eased off her blindfold.

"Lancelot!" sobbed Guinevere, recognizing her rescuer as he lifted her gently onto his horse. The knight in shining armor swept back across the marketplace, like a furious whirlwind, leaving injured and dying knights in his wake. His band of followers met no resistance as they charged after him, heading for his castle.

Over forty knights were killed in the battle on that terrible day. Among them were Sir Tor, Sir Gryflet, and Sir Gawain's two beloved brothers, Sir Gaheris and Sir Gareth.

The loss of so many lives wreaked havoc on the Round Table, as the knights split into opposing camps. Many supported Arthur, and blamed Lancelot for betraying his king and slaughtering so many of his former friends. Those who had lost close comrades were eager to avenge them, and they burned with hatred for Sir Lancelot.

Others, however, were worried about Sir Mordred and his sinister influence on King Arthur. They could not really believe that the knight had caught the lovers together, and they thought Arthur had been foolish to listen to him.

In the end, a large proportion of the Knights of the Round Table abandoned the king, and switched their allegiance to Sir Lancelot. They set off for his castle, miles away from Camelot, to join him there. They sensed that the years of fame and glory for King Arthur and the Knights of the Round Table were nearing their end. Many also had the premonition that the kingdom of Logres was about to be plunged into chaos once more.

That left a third group: Mordred and his followers, who were receiving their instructions from Morgan le Fay. Surveying the wreckage of Arthur's court, once the most powerful gathering of knights in the world, the wicked sorceress saw her chance. She would stop at nothing to bring about the downfall of the Round Table. Sir Lancelot and the king were now enemies. The time for retribution had come.

The last battle

Sir Gawain stared at the young messenger in disbelief. His whole body began to tremble as the terrible truth hit home.

"Both of them?" he said, ashen-faced. The messenger nodded his head solemnly, not daring to look Gawain in the face.

"Dead?" said Gawain.

The messenger's answer was drowned out by an almighty wail of deep despair that tore through the castle walls and out into the valleys below. Shepherds were shaken from their hillside slumbers. Wolves were roused from their lairs and a horrible howling swept down the mountainside and into the villages, to be answered by the baying of every dog for miles around. It was as if the hounds of hell were suddenly unleashed and the kingdom had been ripped savagely apart by the grievous news.

"Sir Gareth and Sir Gaheris were killed by Sir Lancelot this morning," repeated the messenger slowly.

His duty done, he turned to the door. No words could bring back the great knight's beloved brothers or alleviate his sorrow. The simple message had already inflicted a wound too deep to heal.

If Gawain's desperate, driving desire for revenge had not fixed itself so firmly in his heart, like the sword into the stone, and if Arthur had not been so deeply moved by his nephew's grief, and by his own sorrow at the loss of his knights and the betrayal of his wife, perhaps it would have been possible to prevent the terrible chain of events which followed. But when the king rushed in to see what poor, pain-racked creature had uttered that awful cry, and saw his nephew's tortured face screaming for revenge, he knew at once what he had to do.

He quickly called together the remaining Knights of the Round Table and summoned a great army to lay siege to Sir Lancelot's castle.

For fourteen long summer weeks, they camped out around the walls. Every day Arthur would call for silence and challenge Lancelot to fight, and for fourteen long weeks his appeals were met only by the cries of swallows and the calls of corncrakes. On the hundredth day of the siege, when the reapers were bringing the harvest home, a tall figure with long, flowing hair appeared on the battlements. At first Arthur did not recognize his former friend. He looked so gaunt and weary. But Lancelot it was.

"Send your men home, Arthur," he called. "I will not fight my own king."

"We are enemies now, Sir Lancelot," replied Arthur gravely. "And though I would not wish it so, I cannot forgive you for killing my knights, for abducting my wife, or for your betrayal. It's time for justice to be done. Come out and fight."

"I killed your knights to save your queen," shouted Lancelot, "from the horrible death you had sentenced her to. If you could only see reason, you wouldn't listen to the lies of traitors, but would welcome her back with open arms. She did nothing wrong. Why trust Mordred's word rather than hers or mine?"

"Murderer! Liar! Coward!" shrieked a voice from below. It belonged to Sir Gawain. He was bright red in the face and spitting with rage. "You killed my brothers. They were unarmed and you murdered them. You deserve to die, you dog. I want revenge, and I shall never be able to rest until I have it. Come out and fight."

Lancelot tried to reason with Gawain. He told him that he had not recognized Gareth and Gaheris. He said that he did not want to fight, but the grief-stricken knight was implacable. So Lancelot tried one last, desperate appeal to the king:

"Please stop this madness. No good can possibly come of it. We don't have to be set against each other like fighting dogs. I beg of you, Arthur, withdraw."

It is said that the king would have made peace with Lancelot there and then, if it had not been for Gawain's insistence on revenge. But the younger man could not be appeased. He wanted retribution for the deaths of his brothers. With a never-ending stream of invective, he incited everyone around him to challenge Lancelot again and again.

Finally, Lancelot's knights would stand it no longer. A terrible battle ensued. Old friends who had shared so many adventures, so many meals and so many years of glory were set against each other in deadly combat. Many were killed.

Gawain and his men concentrated their attack upon Lancelot, but Lancelot's knights managed to repel them every time. Even in the heat of of the battle Lancelot, the greatest fighter in the land, refused to strike out at his one-time ally.

Finally, Arthur was knocked off his horse by Sir Bors, who was just about to deliver a fatal blow when Lancelot grabbed his arm. "I cannot bear to see my king killed by a friend," he hissed. Then, above the uproar, and still holding Bors firmly by the arm, he shouted to Arthur:

"For God's sake, Arthur, this cannot go on. Please

see reason. Take Guinevere. Take my men. Take my life if you must, but put an end to this hatred. It's breaking my heart."

"I will stop the fighting," said Arthur, remounting his horse, "if Guinevere returns to me, and if you leave my kingdom forever. I cannot find it in my heart to forgive you."

Lancelot agreed to these conditions, and both men ordered their armies to withdraw. Gawain had been wounded, and was too weak and exhausted to protest. Guinevere was led out of the castle. As she crossed the drawbridge, she couldn't resist a final glance back at her beloved knight as he started his preparations for exile in Gaul.

The peace which reigned over Logres after Lancelot's departure from the kingdom was short-lived and troubled. Sir Gawain was inconsolable and brooded relentlessly on his brothers' deaths. Mordred, as usual, leaped on any opportunity to stir up hatred against Lancelot; and finally, so many of the knights were siding with Gawain and Mordred, and demanding revenge, that Arthur had no choice but to declare war on Lancelot again. He summoned his men and set sail for Benwick Castle (Lancelot's new home across the sea in Gaul), leaving Mordred to rule in his absence.

It was the moment Mordred had been waiting for. No sooner had Arthur set sail than he gathered his own army and announced that he had been chosen as heir to the throne, as Arthur had been killed at Benwick. He summoned the Archbishop, and bullied him into performing a hasty coronation. Then he tried to force Guinevere to marry him. Somehow, she managed to escape and sought refuge in a high tower, protected by a few faithful followers. From there, she succeeded in getting this message to Arthur:

COME QUICKLY.
MORDRED HAS USURPED THRONE.
KINGDOM IN DANGER.

As soon as Arthur read this, he started back for

Logres. All that the siege of Benwick had achieved was the death of even more men. Gawain and Lancelot had fought each other three times and each time, Gawain had been wounded. By the time he reached the shores of Logres and tried to mount Gringalet, his old war-horse, he was so weak that he collapsed on the beach. A low groan of pain alerted Arthur. He raced over to see who was in trouble and saw Gawain lying face-down in a pool of bloody water. Arthur turned him over.

"Forgive me," spluttered Gawain, recognizing his uncle. "It's all my fault, the killing and hatred. All so pointless. If it wasn't for me, Lancelot would be here now. I don't want to die his enemy."

"Then tell him," said Arthur, pulling a quill pen from his saddlebag. "Tell me what to say and I'll write a letter to him." So Gawain, through his pain and tears, wrote this letter:

I am about to die from a wound you gave me at Benwick. Please don't let me die your enemy. I know now that my death is my own fault. My futile desire for revenge forced you into battle. I ask for your forgiveness and that you hurry to Arthur's aid with the largest army you can muster. Logres is in danger. Mordred has seized the throne. Arthur needs you.

Come quickly, noble Lancelot.
Gawain

With these words, Gawain took his last breath.

Arthur sat by his side through the long, dark night and cried until dawn finally broke above the majestic chalk cliffs that towered over the beach.

Five nights later, Arthur's army was encamped not far from Lake Avalon, where Arthur had first found Excalibur. Mordred and his men were camped across the plain, less than a mile away. While Arthur was in Gaul, they had marched into the south-west of Logres, seizing people's land and property, and terrorizing anyone who would not join their army.

It was a cold, blustery night and Arthur could not sleep. In the morning, he was to lead his men into battle, a battle which he feared would be his last. If Lancelot, Gawain and all the other Knights of the Round Table had still been with him, he would not have been so fearful of the outcome. But he had lost so many good fighters, and the men he had left were untrained and badly outnumbered.

As he mulled this over, he became aware of a strange, orange glow in the entrance of the tent. He looked up to see a tall, dark figure hovering in the doorway.

"Who's there?" he called.

"It's me, Uncle," said a faint, familiar voice.

"Gawain?" gasped Arthur in amazement. "But I thought you were. . ."

122

"I am, Uncle, but I have come back to warn you."

"Warn me? Of what?"

"If you do battle with Sir Mordred tomorrow, you will both be killed, together with all your men. You must make a truce on whatever terms you can. Within a week, Lancelot will be here and then you'll conquer Mordred. If you fight before then, it will end in disaster. Take heed, Uncle, or you won't have a chance."

"How do you know this?" asked Arthur. The ghostly figure was fading fast.

"Take heed," said the echoing voice again.

"Gawain. . ." called Arthur, but the ghost had vanished.

As soon as it was light, Arthur sent a message to Mordred, asking to meet him halfway between the two camps. Mordred complied, and one hour later the two men approached each other, unaccompanied and unarmed. Mordred agreed to a week's truce, if he could retain the south-west of Logres and have the whole kingdom after Arthur's death. Remembering Gawain's words, Arthur accepted, and both agreed that if any sword were drawn before the week was up, they would take it as a sign that the treaty had been broken.

For two days an uneasy peace reigned over the plain. Arthur paced up and down through the camp, anxiously scanning the horizon for any sign of

Lancelot's arrival. His men kept their eyes fixed firmly on the enemy's distant tents, ready to respond to any sign of provocation.

On the third day, Mordred's men were growing restless. It had become hot and humid, and the prospect of putting on their heavy armor and spending another day in the sun waiting for something to happen was not at all appealing.

One of the knights was putting on his tunic, when he felt a sharp sting on his left foot. Looking down, he saw that he had trodden on a snake. Without thinking, he drew his sword to finish the animal off. Away across the plain, Arthur's men saw the blade flashing in the sunlight. A great cry went up, and within seconds both armies were charging across the plain and into battle.

Centuries later, that last battle was still remembered as the fiercest that Logres had ever seen. All the long day it raged under the hot sun, as men struck out at their enemies in a fevered frenzy of killing. The thirst for blood and the desire for death seemed insatiable, as blow after blow came raining down. Blood-covered swords and dented shields clashed again and again. Toppled knights and horses came crashing down to their deaths on the dusty, sun-baked ground.

At dusk, the clatter of weapons, the neighing of

wounded horses and the groans of dying men gave way to an eerie silence: the silence of death. King Arthur rode among the corpses of his old friends, weeping in despair at the tragic, pointless devastation. Of all his men, only Sir Bedivere and Sir Lucan were left alive, and both were badly wounded.

Suddenly, he caught sight of Mordred, sitting on top of a heap of bodies, carefully wiping the blood off his sword.

"Give me my spear," he said to Lucan under his breath. Gripping the spear like a javelin, Arthur charged at Mordred with a blood-curdling cry.

When Mordred saw him coming, he sprang up and darted forward, sword and shield at the ready, but he could not deflect the weapon, which Arthur thrust at him with such great force that it went straight through his breastplate and into his heart. With one last scream of hatred, anger and pain, Mordred dragged himself forward on the spear, raised his sword in both hands and brought it crashing down on Arthur's head. Then he staggered backwards and fell to the ground with a final, terrible groan.

Arthur sank slowly to his knees. Bedivere and Lucan were there to catch him as he fell, blood gushing from a deep wound where the sword had pierced his helmet.

"Take me to Lake Avalon," he whispered.

With great difficulty, the two wounded knights carried Arthur to the lake and laid him on the grass under an oak tree. Gentle waves lapped the shore in the moonlight. A fine mist covered the water, just as it had when Arthur had first set eyes on the lake, so many years before.

The exertion had been too much for Lucan. His final task over, he lay down next to Arthur, shut his eyes and died. Bedivere sobbed quietly at his side.

"There's no time for tears," said Arthur softly. "I have one more task for you to do. . . the last I may ever ask of you. Take Excalibur, go to the water, throw it in, then tell me what happens. My sight has gone now. Darkness is all I see."

Bedivere took hold of Excalibur and went down to the lake. He heaved the sword high into the air, flinging it as far as he could across the water. Just as it was about to plunge beneath the surface, a small, white hand shot up through the mist and caught it by the handle. The silver blade glistened in the moonlight momentarily before it was drawn slowly down, back beneath the deep, dark waters.

Bedivere staggered back to Arthur and told him what he had seen.

"Then all is well," whispered the king. "And what do you see now?"

"Nothing but mist and moonlight, sir."

"Then look again," croaked Arthur, unable to lift his head. Bedivere peered through the darkness, scanning the mist-covered lake. A gleaming barge was gliding across the water, with a tall figure in flowing white robes standing at the prow.

It was the Lady of the Lake, magically risen from the dead to take Arthur to his resting place.

"Help me to the boat," whispered Arthur.

Bedivere half dragged, half carried the king down to the barge. The lady helped the king on board and laid him down, cradling his wounded head tenderly in her lap.

"Do not leave me, my king," Bedivere pleaded. "What is to become of the kingdom of Logres once you are gone?"

"I must go to the Isle of Avalon," called Arthur. The barge was beginning to drift slowly out into the lake. "But be assured that I will return one day when my kingdom needs me." These were the dying king's final words. Bedivere sat down on the shore and watched, heartbroken, as the barge floated slowly away and disappeared into the night.

Lancelot and his men reached Logres the next day. When he asked for news of Arthur, he was simply told that the king had marched westward. Then he was shown Gawain's grave near the beach. There he spent several hours in prayer and contemplation, thinking about the events that had led to his friend's death. Then he left his men and galloped on towards Avalon. At nightfall, he stopped to shelter in an old abbey deep in the heart of the forest.

As he was led through the cloisters, he passed a group of nuns. One of them uttered a cry and fell to the ground. Lancelot kneeled to help her. The tearful face that stared up at him was strangely familiar. Gone was the long, flowing hair, the embroidered robes and the sweet, innocent smile, but her eyes were as bright as on the day they had first met. It was Guinevere.

Through bitter tears, she told him about everything that had happened: Mordred's treachery, her escape to the tower and of Arthur's last battle, which she had heard about in a message from Bedivere. Lancelot listened horrified, almost unable to believe what he was hearing. Then, with a pitiful wail of sorrow, Guinevere declared that all the death and destruction had been brought about by their love, and that now they must live lives of repentance and vow never to see each other again.

Lancelot would have done anything for Guinevere, but this was almost too much for him to bear. He said a last, tearful goodbye to the woman he loved, and rode off into the forest with a broken heart. He felt as though his life was over. There was nothing left to fight for, and he had no friends left on earth.

One night, many years later, Lancelot dreamed that Guinevere was dying. He rode straight to the abbey the next morning, to discover that she had passed away peacefully in the night. From that moment, Lancelot lost all will to live and refused to eat or drink. Within two weeks he too was dead. Of the other

Knights of the Round Table, only Bedivere survived. He spent the rest of his days living as a hermit, deep in the forest.

So what became of King Arthur? To this day, no one really knows. Some say he died from his wound and was buried on the Isle of Avalon, where a simple gravestone bears the inscription:

HERE LIES ARTHUR,
THE ONCE AND FUTURE KING.

Others say that he was healed by the Lady of the Lake, and now he and Merlin, together with the Knights of the Round Table, are sleeping, deep in a mountain cave somewhere in Wales. One day, they say, when the kingdom is in terrible danger, they will awake from centuries of slumber, and the clanking of armor will be heard once more as King Arthur and the Knights of the Round Table go galloping through the land.

Who's who in the stories

Sir Accolon of Gaul Family: Not known. Career: Lover of Morgan le Fay. Used by her in a plot to kill King Arthur, but Arthur, disguised as Sir Ontzlake, killed Accolon. Personality: Ambitious and brave, but gullible. Status: Knight of Gaul. Attributes: Physically strong. Good fighter.

Sir Agravain Family: Younger brother of Gawain. Career: Joined with Mordred to plot against Arthur. Killed by Sir Lancelot. Personality: Resentful, sly and suspicious. Status: Knight of the Round Table. Attributes: Not a very good knight.

King Arthur Family: Son of King Uther Pendragon and Duchess Igrayne. Brother of Anna, half-brother of Morgan le Fay and foster-brother of Sir Kay. Husband of Guinevere. Career: Brought up by Sir Ector. Removed the sword in the stone to become king. Given the sword Excalibur by the Lady of the Lake. Founded the Round Table at Camelot and ruled Logres. Tricked by Morgan le Fay and betrayed by Mordred, who defeated him in the last battle.

Personality: Kind, tolerant, brave, polite. Status: King of Logres. Attributes: Excellent fighter and good leader.

Sir Bercilak/The Green Knight Family: Husband of the lady of the castle who tested Gawain's honor. Career: Was changed into the Green Knight by Morgan le Fay to test the Knights of the Round Table. Personality: Generous, jovial. As the Green Knight, fierce and brave. Status: Lord of the castle. Attributes: As the Green Knight, able to replace his head after it was cut off.

Sir Ector Family: Foster-father of King Arthur, father of Sir Kay. Career: Brought up Arthur from birth on Merlin's orders. Personality: Patient, reliable, kind. Status: Knight and honorary courtier. Attributes: Trustworthy. Loyal.

Sir Gaheris Family: Younger brother of Sir Gawain, nephew of Arthur, son of King Lot and Queen Anna. Career: Came to Camelot as squire of Gawain. Killed by Lancelot during rescue of Guinevere. Personality: Courageous. Status: Knight of the Round Table. Attributes: Good fighter.

Sir Galahad Family: Son of Lancelot. Career: Brought up by nuns in an abbey in the forest. Brought to Camelot by Lancelot, where he occupied the Siege Perilous (the dangerous seat) at the Round Table.

Personality: Fearless, sinless and invincible. Status: Knight of the Round Table and the best knight of all. Attributes: The perfect knight.

Sir Gareth Family: Younger brother of Sir Gawain, nephew of Arthur, son of King Lot and Queen Anna. Career: Assigned to kitchen duties when he first came to Camelot, until he revealed his true identity and was made a knight. Killed by Lancelot during rescue of Guinevere. Personality: Humble, but brave. Status: Knight of the Round Table. Attributes: Good fighter. Clever.

Sir Gawain Family: Eldest son of King Lot and Queen Anna. Arthur's favorite nephew. Career: Undertook quest for the Green Chapel to prove his worth. Avenged his brothers' deaths by inciting Arthur to fight Lancelot. Fatally wounded by Lancelot in the siege of Benwick. Wrote a letter of reconciliation to Lancelot on his deathbed. Personality: Brave, courteous and honorable, implacable when angry. Status: Knight of the Round Table. Attributes: Excellent knight.

Queen Guinevere Family: Daughter of King Leodegrance and wife of King Arthur. Career: Tried to be loyal to Arthur but was affected by her undying love for her champion Sir Lancelot, who rescued her when she was kidnapped by Sir Melligrance and when she was sentenced to death by Arthur. Became a nun after Arthur's last battle. Personality: Charming, sometimes moody. Status: Queen of Logres. Attributes: Beautiful. Clever.

Duchess Igrayne Family: Wife of Uther, mother of Arthur, Anna and Morgan le Fay. Career: Married Uther after death of her first husband and gave birth to Arthur. Handed baby over to Merlin. Reunited with Arthur when he became king. Personality: Long-suffering and uncomplaining. Status: Duchess of Cornwall. Attributes: Bravery and resilience.

Sir Kay Family: Son of Sir Ector and foster-brother of King Arthur. Career: Brought up alongside Arthur and pretended that he had removed the sword in the stone. Came to Camelot when Arthur became king. Killed in the last battle. Personality: Rude and boastful. Status: Knight of the Round Table. Attributes: Loyalty to Arthur.

The Lady of the Lake Family: Not known. Career: Gave Arthur the sword Excalibur. Raised Lancelot and brought him to Camelot to become a knight. Took Arthur to the Isle of Avalon at the end of his life. Personality: Mysterious. Status: A lake fairy. Attributes: Beauty. Magical powers.

Sir Lancelot du Lake Family: Son of King Ban and Queen Elaine. Father of Sir Galahad. Career: Left near a lake by his mother and raised by the Lady of the

Lake, who later brought him to Camelot on Merlin's orders. Became Guinevere's champion and fell in love with her. Killed forty knights, including Sir Gaheris and Sir Gareth, to rescue Guinevere when she was sentenced to death. Challenged to fight by Sir Gawain, whom he wounded fatally. Exiled to France by Arthur. Upon return to Logres he found out Arthur was dead and Guinevere had become a nun. Died of a broken heart. Personality: Brave, fearless and romantic. Status: Knight of the Round Table. Champion of Queen Guinevere. Attributes: Excellent fighter. Handsome. Noble.

Sir Melligrance Family: Son of King Bagdemus. Career: Kidnapped Guinevere and took her to his castle; she was rescued by Lancelot. Personality: Crafty and cowardly. Status: Knight of the Round Table. Attributes: Weak but cunning.

Merlin Family: Son of Madog Morfryn and Aldan. Career: Adviser to Uther Pendragon, and then to Arthur. Took the baby Arthur from Tintagel Castle to Sir Ector, who brought him up as his own son. Predicted downfall of Camelot. Personality: Mysterious, wise. Status: Sorcerer and prophet. Attributes: Able to cast spells, change shape and predict the future.

Sir Mordred Family: Possibly a nephew of King Arthur. Career: Plotted with Morgan le Fay to bring about Arthur's downfall. Usurped the throne and tried to marry Guinevere while Arthur was in France. Killed by Arthur in the last battle. His final blow fatally wounded Arthur. Personality: Devious, malicious. Status: Knight of the Round Table. Attributes: Good fighter.

Morgan le Fay Family: Daughter of Gorlois and Igrayne, Duke and Duchess of Cornwall. Half-sister of Arthur, wife of Sir Uriens of Gore, mother of Uwain. Career: Learned magic from Merlin. Plotted to kill Arthur and her husband. Changed Sir Bercilak into the Green Knight and sent him to challenge the Knights of the Round Table. Sent Mordred to Camelot to stir up trouble. Personality: Scheming, evil. Status: Sorceress. Attributes: Able to cast spells and change shape.

Sir Pellinore Family: Father of Sir Tor and Sir Percival. Career: Fought Arthur before he became his ally. Killed by Gawain in revenge for killing his father, King Lot of Orkney. Personality: Fierce, belligerent. Status: Knight of the Round Table. Attributes: Fearless and formidable fighter.

Sir Percival Family: Son of Pellinore. Career: Brought up by mother in the forest in Wales until the age of 16, when he met some Knights of the Round Table and decided to become a knight. Went to Camelot and retrieved Arthur's golden goblet when it was stolen. Personality: Brave, sometimes too hasty. Status: Knight of the Round Table. Attributes: A very good knight.

Sir Uriens of Gore Family: Husband of Morgan le Fay. Father of Uwain. Career: Tricked by Morgan le Fay's damsels on enchanted ship. Morgan le Fay tried to kill him, but was thwarted by their son Uwain. Personality: Too trusting. Not very bright. Status: Knight of the Round Table. Attributes: Not one of the better knights.

Sir Uwain Family: Son of Sir Uriens and Morgan le Fay. Career: Stopped his mother from killing his father. Personality: Trustworthy. Status: Knight of the Round Table. Attributes: Dependable.

Another Usborne Classic

VICTORIAN GHOST STORIES

We listened intently. The sound
changed to little pants and fierce sobs,
getting closer and closer, as though a
person in distress were walking to where
we were.

"There's a child out there!" Simson
whispered urgently. "What's a child doing
out so late?"

I remained silent. I knew that it wasn't
a child, not a living one anyway.

Seven spine-tingling stories have been dug up
from the grave and dusted off for this classic selection
of hauntings, howlings and horrors. Enter the world
of ghouls and ghostly apparitions, as the dead return
to torment the living.

Another Usborne Classic

FRANKENSTEIN

FROM THE STORY BY MARY SHELLEY

He made his way to the tank and peered over the rim. There was only the smooth, undisturbed surface of the liquid . . . Confused thoughts and troubled emotions ran through his mind. He had failed, it was true, but maybe that was for the best. He sighed and relaxed slightly. Then, from the liquid, a huge hand shot out to grab him.

As lightning flashes across the night sky, Victor Frankenstein succeeds in the ultimate scientific experiment – the creation of life. But the being he creates, though intelligent and sensitive, is so huge and hideous that it is rejected by its creator, and by everyone else who meets it. Soon, the lonely, miserable monster turns on Victor and his family, with terrifying and tragic results.

Another Usborne Classic

DRACULA

FROM THE STORY BY BRAM STOKER

When the other passengers on the stagecoach found out where Jonathan was going, they stared at him in astonishment. Then they started whispering in Transylvanian and Jonathan heard some words that he knew: pokol and vrolok. The first word meant hell, and the second . . . Jonathan shivered. It meant vampire.

When Jonathan Harker arrives at creepy Castle Dracula in Transylvania, he has no idea what to expect, but all too soon his host's horrible nocturnal habits have him fearing for his life. . . This is the story of a battle against the forces of evil, as the eccentric Professor Van Helsing and his brave young friends take on the vilest vampire in the world.